ANSLEY CALLOWAY

Begging Baby

First edition

This book was professionally typeset on Reedsy.
Find out more at reedsy.com

For the people pleasers, I hope you find someone that takes care of you, especially when you forget to put yourself first.

Contents

Chapter 1

Reese

The first, and often the only, breath of air in my day was always dedicated to the sacred act of making coffee. Those ten minutes belonged to me, and me alone. I doubled the standard coffee grounds, so when poured over ice, the coffee never tasted like watered down dirt. Then I added enough cream to make it look like chocolate milk. A dash of cinnamon. And a heaping dollop of whipped cream, for good health. That was the morning ritual I clung to. Every. Single. Day.

As the coffee began dripping into the glass pot, I took the time to ponder one of my favorite free response prompts to give my kids. What would *I* do if I had an extra hour in my day? Try to make that apple pie recipe saved on my Pinterest board from scratch. Or maybe go to one of those dance workout classes the pretty history teacher down the hall talked about every lunch break. Even better, go for a walk on that deserted trail behind my apartment building that runs along the lake.

The smell of coffee got stronger, and so did my daydreams. If I wasn't a teacher, what would I be doing right now? Sleeping. For hours longer. Only to wake up at nine, and decide to redecorate my entire home for autumn (which is distinctly different from decorating for Halloween). In that scenario, I married rich.

The stream of coffee stopped abruptly, so I pushed up from the off-white laminate counter I was leaning against. Carefully, I picked the coffee pot up to start pouring. Being an artist would be fun, I could wear clothes stained from paint, and be able to make a doctor appointment anytime I wanted. Entrepreneurship had always appealed-

A gravelly voice interrupted both my thoughts and the calming sound of Colbie Caillat.

"Do you always sleep in my jersey?"

My hand froze, but the ice continued to melt in my giant blue to-go cup in front of me.

After pausing in place, I yanked the piping hot coffee pot away from the cup. I shrieked. A very girly, gasping shriek. Turning my head to the side, I saw the giant form of my best friend filling out nearly every inch of my kitchen's doorway. His body took a relaxed stance, as if he spent every morning leaning against my door frame.

I tracked his gaze trailing down the jersey I wore until it reached my bare legs. My back straightened, and my hands pulled the oversized shirt down to cover as much skin as possible.

"And without anything else underneath?" His voice held blatant amusement, and his jaw ticked the way it always did when he was trying not to smile. Jerk.

My eyes dramatically pointed to the side to ask him to get out of my way. I wanted to retreat to my bedroom and die in peace. Ignoring my discomfort, he seemed to be comfortable with staying put, his dark brown eyes fixated on

2

me and sparkling from restrained laughter. With my voice box suddenly incapable of functioning, I had no choice but to glare at him until he moved reluctantly out of my way.

His footsteps on the tile filled the heavy, awkward silence. Ryan gently grabbed the coffee pot from the counter and finished pouring until my coffee cup was full. Too full. Now, to put in the right amount of creamer or whipped cream, I'd have to pour some out. *I hate wasting coffee.*

The thought brought my voice back. "I gave you that key in case of emergencies, not when I'm home and you could've knocked."

His back turned to me, and I admired the view of his broad shoulders stretching out his white t-shirt. Another beat of silence reminded me I was staring, so I took a step back to put distance between us. My best friend was attractive. Anyone who could see was aware of that, so I tried not to let myself stare any longer than necessary. It was best for all parties involved.

Grabbing a mug that read 'World's Best Teacher', he poured his own coffee without adding any ice or creamer. He faced me again as he lifted the steaming mug to his lips to take a sip. I waited for him to wince, and while Ryan had a great poker face, he still grimaced a bit. I felt a little justified after he intruded on my moment of peace.

"I wasn't sure if you were asleep or something. The sun isn't even up." His tired eyes trailed from mine down my body, back to my bare legs. "Maybe I should've knocked."

Suddenly reminded of my current state, I walked to my bedroom backward so Ryan couldn't see my ass. We held eye contact, and I was grateful his eyes didn't stray again.

"Yeah, next time, maybe knock," I squeaked.

In the bedroom mirror, my cheeks flushed red as I hurried to get dressed and ready for the day. Routinely, I pinned my hair back so it was out of my face, shrugged on my sunny yellow dress that flowed around my ankles, and sat on my bathroom counter to start my makeup.

Ryan Summers breaking into my apartment at six in the morning on a Friday was perplexing. I steadied my hand by leaning my arm against the bathroom mirror. Usually, getting mascara on while still half asleep was tricky, but I felt as if I'd already drank a full cup of coffee.

I had never known Ryan to wake up this early for anything other than volleyball, and the season was over. Maybe he finally broke that bad habit. While I would still call him my best friend, we didn't see each other nearly as much as we used to. It was kind of difficult to make time when he lived halfway across the world six months out of the year.

Returning to my bedroom, my bright pink earrings sat in my overflowing dish of colorful jewelry on my dresser. I jabbed my earlobe a couple of times before getting the second one in as I exited my bedroom.

Ryan sat back on my couch and faced the sunrise. Just like I liked to do when I had extra time, with my coffee mug in hand. I sighed and sat down next to him after grabbing my comfiest loafers to slip on.

"So what exactly are you doing here?" I asked.

His head turned, and he took in my new state of dress. We looked like polar opposites now. He completely lacked color with his dark brown hair, white t-shirt, and baggy black cargo pants. One of the corners of his mouth lifted up at the sight of my colorful outfit before he spoke.

"I need a place to stay."

4

I scoffed. "What happened to your high-rise with a built-in butler?" He had his very own, especially nice, apartment that was paid for by his athletic contract, located next to his training facility in the city. It was one of the perks he had for signing on to the league. When he invited me to visit, I had to pick my jaw up off the floor over the view from his floor to ceiling windows.

"It's a cleaning service. I've never had a butler."

"Close enough," I muttered. "There's no one named Jeeves hiding around here." My eyes strayed to look around the messily painted beige room that had clearly been a landlord's special.

"I don't need a butler, Reese." His quiet tone brought my head up to meet his gaze. "It makes sense for me to stay in town for a while with everything going on. My sister's graduation, Nick and Charlotte's wedding, and my mom has some dirtbag new man."

He paused to wave his hand in front of my face as my attention strayed to collect my laptop and put it in my bag. "Are you listening?"

There were plenty of better places to stay in Rosewood than on my couch that was little more than a loveseat. Ryan's six feet and four inches had no way of fitting on the tiny furniture. But if he felt so inclined, I wasn't one to say no to a friend in need.

"Sure, knock yourself out trying to fit on this thing." I patted the sofa lovingly before standing up and continuing to gather all of the things I needed for the day.

My mind went into autopilot as I started rambling off my guest script, "You're welcome to anything in the fridge other than the jello cake. That's for a lesson I'm doing tomorrow.

There are sheets, blankets, and extra pillows in the closet if you want to go back to sleep and-"

"Reese. I've been here before, I know where everything is." I turned to find him much closer than I expected as he watched me pack my bag. "Thank you."

I nodded quickly. "Okay, then have a good day. I'll be back before dark." Pausing for a moment to take a look at him, I debated calling in sick. Was this a call for help? Asking for a favor was very unlike him. "Will you be okay on your own?"

He gave me a judgy look before raising his mug. "I'm a grown man, and I have everything I need. Have a good day at work."

And with that, I was confident enough to go to school, not to mention, out of time to debate staying. I hurriedly grabbed my keys and shuffled out the door before offering Ryan a few more goodbye's out of habit. Halfway down the carpeted hall, I rummaged around in my bag with one hand to make sure I had everything. A sigh escaped me as I realized I yet again left something behind.

I turned to run back for the forgotten items. My door opened quicker than I meant for it to and obnoxiously banged into the door stopper. Immediately spotting what I needed on the kitchen counter, I snatched up the plastic baggies. One was filled with peas, and the other with kibble. Then I gave one last quick wave to Ryan.

My apartment was near the center of town, so the building was one of the oldest in Rosewood. It did have a lot of character, the red brick and eclectic tiles that made up the lobby being some of my favorite features. The price was also teacher-friendly, but it was in desperate need of renovation.

Once I made my way outside, I found one of my main draws to the place other than its cheap rent; the two rivaling families. Approaching the ducks first, I scattered peas along the grass near the bank of the small lake that resided next to my apartment complex. The ducks quieted up and raced to be the first to eat their snack.

My eyes rolled at a loud hiss behind me, and I turned to see the calico cat I lovingly referred to as 'Mama'. "Hold your horses, please," I cooed lovingly.

Two much smaller cats appeared out of the bushes as I approached. The multi-colored siblings sat patiently while I poured kibble into Mama's bowl first, and then the bowl they insisted on sharing. There were a few other cats that hung around my apartment complex, but they were much more skittish, so I left a final bowl a bit further away from the main three cats.

A quack shortly followed by another hiss grabbed my attention. The ducks never understood the territory line that the cats seemingly decided upon by themselves. I herded the crowd of ducks away from the shed and closer to the shoreline of the water before heading to school in my silver Toyota.

At the end of my morning lesson, I finally had a chance to sit down and take my first sip of coffee. Bitter sludge overwhelmed my senses. Pitiful choking filled the air as I tried clearing my throat to get the awful taste out. This morning I must have put on the lid without fixing Ryan's grave error, so I was left with plain black iced coffee. Yuck.

A few students looked up from their homework to check if I was dying. Doing my best to remove the sour look from my face, I waved them off and grabbed my emergency water bottle from my bag to wash down the disgusting aftertaste. I chanced a look at the clock and inwardly grimaced before bracing myself for an incredibly long day.

Halfway through lunch, I broke and bought a soda from the vending machine. The only thing harder than teaching high school was teaching high school caffeine-free. If I couldn't be hopped up on sugary coffee, the next best thing was a sugary soda.

The clicking of heels sounded in the hallway, and I had the dreaded feeling that someone was about to interrupt my lunch break. I capped my blue pen and took another big drink of my soda. The knock that followed the silence of her heels was swift, and the door swung open before I could even call out for her to come in.

"I have more research for you to do if you don't mind, Ms. Finch," my principal so graciously stated.

Her perfectly manicured nails dropped a plain binder on my desk. It fell right on top of the quizzes I was grading before she walked in. One more thing for my metaphorical plate. And my physical desk. Barely any of the wood laminate desktop could be seen due to the piles of papers added to my usual assortment of necessities– like my much needed coffee cup.

My polite smile felt heavier in her presence. "Sure, is there a time limit on this one? I have some company visiting this weekend-"

"Monday will be just fine, thank you. And if you could get it to me first thing?" Her tone implied it as a question, but I knew it, in fact, was not. "I have an important meeting with the director that afternoon."

"Of course, I'll include the talking points as usual." There goes my weekend.

"That will be good, Ms. Finch. Enjoy your time off."

Her frown lines deepened as she grimaced instead of smiled. I wasn't sure if she knew the difference. Her heels click-clacked out of my room, and I listened to them retreat down the hall since she left my door wide open. Sighing, I looked around at all of the work she left me to enjoy doing in my 'time off'. Another gulp of my soda gave me just enough courage to pick up my pen and continue grading.

* * *

After school, I found Beth outside waiting on the steps. This year, she moved up to eleventh grade, so she was no longer my student, but there were some kids that I liked to keep in touch with. She was visibly very pregnant now, leaning against the step behind her, stretching out her back.

Her head raised as I approached, and her sandy blonde hair fell away from her eyes while she smiled at me. "Hello, Ms. Finch," she chirped.

I greeted her with a quick hug before reaching down to grab her bag for her while she stood up. Her hand rested on her lower back. "I'm so sorry to ask, but would you mind giving me a ride again? My mom is busy, and I need to go to work."

"Of course, I'm always happy to help. Plus, you know I love to visit Charlotte," I answered cheerily.

Beth worked for one of my best friends, who just so happened to own my favorite coffee shop. This was the turn of events my day desperately needed. I swung her backpack over my free shoulder that wasn't carrying my own bag, and we walked to the teacher's parking lot together.

Brewing Pages was looking as adorable as ever. Marigolds were overflowing from the garden boxes on either side of the front door, and there was a beautiful painting on the window of a tree with falling leaves. It perfectly matched the scene around us on Main Street, a few trees' leaves had just begun turning color and some fell with the breeze.

"Did you do this?" I pointed to the paint on the window while I held the door open for Beth.

She smiled shyly. "Do you like it? I don't paint trees often, so it's not my best work."

"It's so lovely, Beth. You're very talented. Are you still taking art classes this year?" I set her bag down next to the counter where Charlotte was serving a customer.

Her lip fell into a pout while she started tying up her hair. "No, I needed to double up my math classes since I'm trying to finish a semester early next year." She smiled over at Charlotte in greeting. "At least I can still do paintings for the shop."

I nodded encouragingly. "Or, I'm sure there are clubs or classes somewhere, if you ever wanted to take more art classes after you graduate and the baby is born."

She touched her stomach lovingly, "I hope she enjoys making art too."

"If she's anything like you, I'm sure she will."

Charlotte's messy bun bounced with her as she walked over to our end of the counter. "Well this is a surprise, I was beginning to think you were avoiding me."

I smiled widely at her and went in for a hug, even though she wasn't a hugger. "The start of school is always a chaotic time for me. I'm sorry for being a horrible friend."

She laughed at my dramatics, replied with a playful eye roll, and spoke, "You're allowed to work, Reese. I'll find a way to forgive you."

"Okay, great. Because I *really* need a coffee, please."

Her loud sigh nearly covered up the sound of Beth giggling at our antics. "If I have to," Charlotte said with feigned

10

exhaustion.

After she made my drink, she came and sat with me for an hour while Beth worked. We did some much needed catching up as I relished in the sweet taste of my beloved drink. It wasn't exactly the same as when I made it, but it was the closest anyone else had ever gotten.

"Oh, and would you be able to watch the dogs for us while we go on our vacation? It would be in a few months, obviously, but I thought I would start asking around now."

I set down my cup and nodded excitedly. "Of course, you know I love them." I had no idea how I would house the two very large dogs in my apartment— one of which was still an overexcited puppy, or find the time to take care of them. But I couldn't say no to Charlotte, or the image of two sweet puppy faces needing a place to stay.

"It will be nice to have some company," I offered. Which reminded me of my current company waiting for me back at home.

Charlotte gave my hand a quick squeeze as her way of saying thank you. "You're the best, I knew I gave you all those free drinks for a reason," she teased.

I laughed into my hand. "I will never stop owing you." Grabbing my keys, I began putting on my knit cardigan. "I should get back home to my surprise guest before he gets stir crazy."

Her eyebrows raised with the corners of her mouth. "He? Is it Ryan?"

"Why is that your first guess? As if he stays with me often?" I questioned accusingly.

She relaxed into her chair and crossed her arms with a knowing look. "I just think if you were to have any man stay over, it would be Ryan."

Well, *we are friends,* but Ryan and I weren't exactly sleepover friends. When he visited in the past, he always stayed with his mom. I wasn't sure why this time was any different.

"He'll probably just be here for the weekend. No need to get all excited."

Charlotte ignored my dismissal of the subject. "You know, my therapist would refer to this as a 'doorknob confession', we've been talking for over an hour and you *just* now mention this?"

"Like I said, it's a casual thing. I think he just didn't want to stay with his mom." I gave her a pointed look. "And all of our nosey friends are definitely not going to be weird about it. Right?"

She pretended to zip her lips. "Mum's the word."

* * *

The sunset reflected a painting of colors across the lake when I pulled into my parking lot. I took a second to watch before getting out and going up to face my childhood best friend. Did he really want to stay with me? Surely it was all a big joke.

My keys loudly clanged against my door as I unlocked it. I crept in slowly and made sure to announce my presence with a loud 'I'm home'. Which felt very weird to do. My entire adult life I lived alone, so the phrase felt a little foreign. Instead of a returned greeting, I was met with silence. I knew better than to trust that, though, since Ryan seemed to have a fun habit of sneaking up on me lately.

The apartment seemed untouched since I left it that morning. I flicked on lights as I walked through and plopped my bag on the floor with a loud thunk. Was I daydreaming a bit too much this morning? There was no sign anyone else had ever even been here. I walked to the sink to find proof, and there was the rinsed out mug he used this morning. At least I wasn't crazy.

As I pulled out my phone to text him, a firm knock sounded on my door. I waited a second, expecting him to come in on his own. When he didn't, I got up and answered the door. My neck craned to meet his eyes. They were brown, but also looked hazel in some lighting. Now was one of those times.

"May I come in?" he asked dryly.

I flustered at his question. After a certain amount of hours in a day spent dealing with teenagers, my brain shut down and forgot all manners. I was totally staring. Jolting back a step and swinging the door wide open, I gestured with the grandeur of a clown.

"Please, come in."

He nodded quickly before walking past. "Are you alright? You've been awfully jumpy."

"You're the one who broke into my apartment this morning, I believe I have a right to act a little jumpy."

He swiftly pulled his gym bag up and over his head and set it down next to my loveseat, which was about six feet across from the front door. The deadpan look he often wore was set in stone as he answered simply, "You gave me a key."

Sometimes I wondered how Ryan managed to attract women, given that he had the social graces of an elephant. I decided to choose my battles for tonight and dropped the conversation. I bent down to reach into my bag for the papers I still needed to grade, but the strap of the bag popped open, and everything came spilling out.

Exasperated, I sat down on the floor and let out a long sigh. What shit luck. In my ten second long pity party, Ryan sat next to me and began organizing the papers into piles again. He took a few rogue paperclips and started securing them together.

"Do you have to grade all of these this weekend? Who gives out quizzes on a Friday?" he teased gently.

I smiled regretfully and reached for the piles he put together. "I gave them out yesterday, I'm just grading them today." I stood and brought the quizzes from my last two classes to the table. "Are you actually sleeping here tonight?"

He frowned and stared at me from across the small room. "I intended on it, but if you're busy I can get a hotel in Somerset or something."

My eyebrows raised. "I'm not too busy, I just wanted to make sure you weren't joking." Usually, Friday nights were dedicated to pizza and grading, but I could finish these tomorrow after Ryan left. "Does Sal's sound good?"

He sat next to me and reached for one of my student's papers. "Sounds great, I have cash." His legs stretched out awkwardly, so I moved to push the table in front of us further away to give him more space. "Can I help with these?" he asked.

Distracted by putting in our pizza order on my phone, I shook my head slowly. "No, that's okay."

Out of the corner of my vision, I caught a glint of the whites of his eyes. "You were going to grade these. Am I supposed to just watch you?"

"I can just do it later."

My back straightened so I could reach the papers to put them back in my bag. His hand reached out to cover mine completely, and I did my best to act normal at the contact.

Ryan wasn't exactly the physically affectionate type.

"I'll help, we can knock this out before the pizza even gets here." When I didn't move to agree, he gently lifted my hand and put it back in my lap. "What are these? Short answer? Just give me the answers and I can mark it for you."

"This is silly, I'll just do it-"

"Rock, paper, scissors, I win, and we do it together. You win, and I'll let it go. We can watch one of those painfully cringe reality TV shows you're always finding."

I cheered up at the sound of that. "Deal. Don't act like you haven't liked every single one I force you to watch."

We held our hands out and recited the classic phrase. I went with my lucky choice, scissors. Everyone always chose to go paper on the first round, but scissors were clearly the superior starting point. I watched his right hand with anticipation as it smacked his opposite hand in the shape of a rock. Drats.

Chapter 2

Ryan

Reese picked scissors first in every game of rock paper scissors that she played since she was fourteen. Maybe even earlier than that, but we were definitely in middle school when I first realized. I used that knowledge to my advantage at every opportunity. My first night staying in her apartment, I leveraged the game twice. Once to help her with her work, and the other to convince her I could sleep on her couch. What a mistake that was.

There were few times that I could remember being annoyed with my height in my life. In fact, it was one of my best traits, it helped my career as an athlete immensely. A few extra inches gave me valuable reach over other players when it came to slamming the ball down on their side of the volleyball court.

Staying at Reese's was one of those few aforementioned times. De-curling myself from her so-called couch, which I would have referred to as an oversized chair if I knew it wouldn't make her insist on letting me take her bed, was slow and painful. The ache in my body felt like it went through my muscles and into my bones.

Methodically, I stretched out all of my limbs the best I could on the small living room floor, taking extra care of my left shoulder and groaning inwardly every step of the way. Reese's humming pulled me out of my stretching routine, so I followed her voice and made my way to the kitchen. She seemed to have no awareness of her surroundings. I would be lying if I said I didn't find it oddly endearing.

Seconds ticked by as I watched her pour her coffee into a ridiculously oversized thermos with a small smile on her face. She wore polka dot pajama pants paired with one of our high school's t-shirts, and I wondered if she was only wearing pants for my sake. Her humming pulled me out of my thoughts, and I did my best to consider how to alert her to my presence without scaring her.

My genius mind came up with nothing other than pretending to cough. It ended up sounding like I was choking to death, but it certainly caught her attention.

The creamer she was reaching for was knocked over by her elbow as she nearly snapped her neck to face me. "Jesus Christ, do I need to put a damn bell on you?" she said while laughing in disbelief.

I couldn't help but snicker a bit. Maybe I needed to start stomping around her apartment so she would know where I was, but then again, I doubted she would be aware of that either. I could dress up in a clown suit, and Reese would still be oblivious.

"You need to get your hearing checked, old woman." Jumping in to clean up the spill for her, I let her finish making her coffee. I heard her grumbling under her breath as she found a mug and poured mine black.

"I'm only a couple years older than you."

17

She grumpily pushed my coffee toward me, so I grabbed it slowly. I was planning on going out for coffee this morning since it was so awful yesterday, but it felt rude to turn down anything given to me by Reese. Especially when she already had a rare frown on her face.

"Not showing any support for the Vipers today," I mumbled teasingly, more to myself than to Reese. I took a long drink of coffee while her cheeks flushed. "The coffee tastes good."

She grunted and led the way back to the nightmare of a couch she owned. "It was double strength yesterday. I'm surprised you were able to sleep fourteen hours later after drinking that black."

Clearly nothing I had to say this morning was humoring her, so I resorted to silence. We sat across from each other on the couch. I watched as Reese put her legs up and folded herself into the corner of it to look out the only decent sized window in her apartment. Again, I found myself wondering if this was what she did every morning.

Her curly hair was pushed up onto her head with a clip that barely held the bulk of her hair together, in the early morning sun it almost resembled a halo of curls. The freckles that speckled her face were much more visible without the makeup she usually wore, and her lips lacked the smile that she almost always displayed. My favorite smile. While I loved it, it was also nice to see her without it sometimes, she seemed more real. Like an angel brought down to Earth.

"Are you hungry? I can make us breakfast," Reese offered.

I shook my head, noting that her coffee was now empty and the sun was fully risen. "Let's go to the diner, let Nick make us some food."

Reese was a decent cook, but I didn't want her to have to

make me breakfast after inserting myself into her apartment the last two days. And my culinary skills began and ended at bland chicken and rice with frozen vegetables.

"Okay, let me get ready. Do you want to shower first?"

"Go ahead, I'll take one after you."

After waiting thirty minutes, having Reese instruct me to flush the toilet twice in a row, and turning the water on and off three times to get the hot water to come back on, I came to the conclusion that Reese needed to move. But that was a discussion for another time. Preferably, when I had food in my stomach and without pain shooting through my shoulder.

The diner's doorbell chimed as I pulled it open, and Reese practically skipped through the door in front of me to land on her favorite stool of Nick's bartop. He gave us a quick nod from the kitchen and made his way over to us. In hand, he had a blueberry muffin on a plate that he slid in front of Reese without question.

"You're in town again, Summers?" Nicholas Reid was a few years older than me and one of my old teammates from high school. While a frequent pain in my ass, he was also one of my closest friends. If I even had those anymore.

I leaned and rested my arm on the back of Reese's stool. "Yeah, for the entire off season this time."

Reese coughed into her muffin and sat up straighter, accidentally brushing my arm. "You are?"

I stared at her out of confusion. Had I not told her exactly that when I asked to stay with her? Nick cut our staring match short though when he snorted and laid a hand on the bar.

His eyes held pure joy, and I knew he had about a million jokes prepared about how I was 'so in love with Reese' and 'hopeless'. Hopeless was definitely the right word, but I knew

Reese and I were only ever going to be friends.

Instead of throwing a few blows to my ego, he asked me what I wanted to eat and left it at that. Halfway through my heavenly plate of eggs and bacon– Nick was a menace, but he was a damn good cook– Reese's phone rang, and I had a feeling this would be the end to our morning together.

Through a series of hums and okays, I gathered that Reese had some crisis she needed to solve, so I gestured for her to put her wallet away as she reached for it.

"I'm so sorry. I-"

I cut her off. "Don't worry about it, do you need help?"

Reese's head shook quickly. "No, sorry, I just totally forgot that I promised one of the mom's from the school that I could help sew this dress for a vow re-"

"It's okay Reese, go save the day."

"Are you sure? I can drive you somewhere if you want."

Nick stepped in and slapped my arm across the counter. "Don't worry, Reese. I'll take care of Summers here. It is Saturday after all, and he could use some reminding of who taught him to play volleyball."

My eyes rolled out of habit, but I forced myself to try and smile while I gave Reese a wave goodbye. Although, it felt more like a wince than a smile. Nick hit my bad shoulder in his dumb attempt at showing he would 'take care of me'.

I turned my head at the sound of the door closing to see a blur of Reese hurry off to her car. "Aren't you working? The customers might not appreciate volleyballs being served where they eat."

"Only for the next twenty minutes, then you're all mine Summers." I grunted as he walked away and rushed to shovel more food in my mouth.

Saturdays in Rosewood were for volleyball. It started back in high school when we would get together on our own to play for fun and try out new moves. I wasn't around much anymore, but there was always something comforting about knowing no matter where I was, the court in Rosewood was still getting some use once a week.

Hanging out with the guys only got more isolating by the year, though. These were people I grew up with, friends I've had for over a decade, and yet the longer I knew them, the less I knew about them. Even Ashton, who also went the pro-athlete route, was so infatuated with his kid and wife that I didn't know how to talk to him anymore.

But thank fuck for Will Rose. In high school, I thought he was a complete asshole. He didn't talk to anyone more than he had to, but I respected him for it. He always took games more seriously than anyone else in the room. The older I got, the more I related to him, and lately it was a bit more than I would like to admit.

Will walked up to us as soon as we got to the beach. Rosewood volleyball practice was usually done inside a gym, but every now and then, they liked to switch it up and hold a practice in the sand.

"Please, for my sanity, go look at your brother's ultrasound pictures. It has been twenty minutes and I have no idea what else to say about a blurry picture that somewhat resembles an alien," Will directed at Nick.

"On it."

Nick might tease his twin brother about being a softie, but he was just as guilty. The second he walked over and Ashton shoved the photo in his face, his smile widened. That man might not want kids, but he sure as hell fell over his feet for

21

his nieces.

Something in me turned annoyed while watching them. Jealous, almost. A part of why I was back here in Rosewood ate at me deep in my soul; I wanted a home. A family. And for now, a dorky band of misfit losers obsessed with volleyball would have to suffice.

"How long are you staying in town this time?" Will asked.

I kneeled down to re-tie my shoelaces. "A few months. I'm going to try staying until I decide on my next contract."

"Where are you staying? With your mom?"

I laughed awkwardly, mentally preparing myself for the teasing to commence. "Actually, I'm staying with Reese."

Standing up to my full height, I chanced a glance sideways at him. His head was tilted in a way that told me he saw through my nonchalant tone. "Isn't her apartment like two feet wide?"

"Yeah, you're definitely right about that. And the appliances aren't much better, I need to find her a new place before I go. Do you know of anywhere?"

He continued staring through my soul with his dark eyes until he sighed, seemingly too tired to start on the usual 'Ryan and Reese sitting in a tree' comedic act. Although Will had never really been one to start the dumb jokes.

"I'll ask around," he offered. I nodded before we both headed onto the sand. A gust of wind hit us, and I breathed in the salty sea air that reminded me so much of home. Nostalgia wasn't something that washed over me often, and in its absence, I started to crave it.

A very grainy picture was shoved in my face as soon as I was within arms reach of Ashton. "Look at my kid. Pretty cool, huh? We're having another girl."

The dopey smile on his face made my eyes widen before I

took a good look at the picture. "Definitely looks like a Reid to me."

Ashton's eyebrows furrowed at my flat tone. "What the hell is that supposed to mean, Summers?"

I waved him off and gestured to take the volleyball from Nick. My sore shoulder would have to suck it up for the day. "Let's play, shall we?"

Saturday volleyball practice was officially a wrap for me after landing a dive in the sand on my bad shoulder. Thankfully, the day was already winding down. We went for a quick sprint along the water to decide who would be paying for drinks at the closest dive bar, and headed out.

Nick dropped me off at Reese's around sunset, and I made the effort to knock. Not hearing any signs of life, I called her instead since I would much rather be with her than stuck in her tiny apartment alone any longer.

"Hey, how did volleyball practice go?" her voice was breathy.

I checked to make sure Reese's door was locked before walking back down the hallway to get to my car. "It was good, where are you? I knocked."

"Oh, I'm just uh-" A bang followed up by a muttered curse from Reese. "You remember Ms. Oatley right? She lives in our old neighborhood. I was visiting my mom, and I found her trying to move all of this dirt on her own for her garden so-"

Pinching the bridge of my nose to keep from raising my voice, I cut her off. "Where does Ms. Oatley live?"

* * *

Turned out Ms. Oatley was creating an entire damn mountain

in her backyard. If her gardening endeavors worked out, she had enough space to feed all of Rosewood. The heat was no joy either, the last days of summer had dragged out for too long. I grabbed my damp shirt to wipe off my forehead for some relief. On my last wheelbarrow trip, I set it down with a thud to rejoin Reese and her new best friend who were chatting with lemonade on the porch.

"You're all set, Ms. Oatley."

The older woman stood up faster than I expected, and her arms weaved their way around me in a tight hug. "Thank you, young man. Now I know why all those old bats at my salon talk about you, a true *gentleman*."

"Glad we could help," I responded while sliding out of her grip.

I gave her a nod before gesturing to Reese. She would stay there all night chatting up the town, and I was dead tired. The two said their goodbyes and well wishes. I led Reese down the porch steps with one last wave to the older woman. Ms. Oatley, not Reese, to be clear.

"I can't believe you were planning on doing that yourself," I sighed and pulled up my shirt to wipe off my face again.

She gave me her best smile with a hand on my bicep. "You could have at least let me carry some of it. I was the one who offered to help in the first place."

I set my hand on her lower back when she stumbled in the dark. My pace slowed to make sure Reese didn't trip again. A few more bags of dirt caught my eye when I turned to her, so I quickly jogged over to grab them and put them in Ms. Oatley's garage in case it rained.

Reese's gaze followed my face as I walked back to her. "You flinched."

"What?" I began herding her back toward my car.

"When you picked those up, you flinched. Are you hurt?" Her voice was insistent. When Reese found something that was broken, she had to fix it right away.

I sighed, knowing she wouldn't let this go. "I've been playing beach volleyball all day, and then pretended I was a landscaper for the last few hours. Give me a break."

"Is it the sofa? I knew it was going to be painful for you to sleep on that damn couch!"

I couldn't help the chuckle that escaped me. There was no energy left in my body to defend that sad excuse of a couch. I opened the car door for her and gestured for her to sit while she was silently stewing over all the ways she could rectify the situation.

"Are you staying with me again tonight?" she asked. This again. I thought she already agreed to that, but she seemed to be facing some kind of retrograde amnesia with all of the bullshit on her to-do list.

The ignition hummed and I sat back. "I thought you already said it was okay for me to." Maybe she didn't want me to stay with her and this was Reese's way of kindly asking me to get out. "I can find somewhere else if you want your couch back."

"No, I don't mind you sleeping over. But I thought you were joking-" she let out an incredulous laugh. "Why would you sleep on my tiny ass couch when you could stay in a hotel nearby or with your mom?"

My shoulders shrugged, and I looked around for her car on the dimly lit street. The prospect of sleeping in a hotel to visit my own hometown was even more depressing when it came from her mouth. Not to mention, she clearly needed someone looking out for her if she was regularly finding herself doing back-breaking manual labor in the middle of the night.

"She has a new loser staying with her this week. And I came to Rosewood to spend time with my friends. You're always busy. Seemed like the easiest way."

A beat of silence drew my gaze to her. One look at her face, and I tried to remember when I said I kicked a puppy, because she looked back at me with tears welling up. It was pure pity swimming around in those big brown eyes.

"You *missed* me! You big sap."

She threw her arms around me awkwardly with the middle console in between us, and I did my best to relax into the hug. "Where's your car, bug?"

Her arms tightened and then quickly released me to swipe under her eyes before pointing down the street. "You're so sleeping on the bed tonight," she murmured. I stared her down and didn't push the subject any further.

When we got out of our cars at the parking lot of her apartment, she wandered off to make sure the stray cats she mothered were safe in their little cat houses for the night. I stood a few feet away wondering who took care of her while I was gone.

Chapter 3

Reese

I knew I shouldn't have let him sleep on that damn couch. I pointed for Ryan to sit down on said forsaken sofa while I went to grab some lotion. My TV played openings for various shows while Ryan flipped through to find something he wanted to watch. Sitting back down beside him, I waved my hand around to gesture for him to take off his shirt.

His eyes narrowed first at the bottle of lotion and then back at my hand. "What exactly are you trying to do here, Reesey piece?"

I lightly smacked his shoulder and to my displeasure he actually flinched. "I'm going to massage it, dummy. Take off your shirt."

Although the selfish part of my brain wanted to sneak a peek, I turned away politely to give him some semblance of privacy. When he plopped his shirt down in my lap, I was careful to keep my eyes trained on only his shoulder, but his snort of air yanked my gaze up to his face. Never had I seen a look so smug.

Choosing to ignore whatever dumb comment he was surely

thinking about my prudish behavior, I rubbed my hands together with some of the lotion. The calming scent of cherry blossom hit my nose. My eyes couldn't help but trail down a little to his bicep as I started massaging, his well defined muscles moved with my hands as I tried to firmly work out whatever knots the couch had created.

"Eyes up here, ma'am." The smug look was back.

"Just pick something for us to watch, will you? Your whole back feels like one giant knot of a bunch of smaller knots that were knotted together by a very determined seaman." My cheeks warmed a little at his accusation, but he wasn't going to embarrass me into giving in.

"A seaman?" He was actively laughing at me now, I felt a little guilty about the flip my heart did at the sight. It wasn't often I saw genuine joy on his face anymore. "I think you mean a sailor."

"Sailor or seaman. Same thing," I grumbled.

He kept his head turned to continue looking directly at my face, even though the action movie that he decided on began to play. "I'm glad you still do that," he mumbled fondly.

I gave him a stern look, not expecting to enjoy his answer. "What?"

"Make up words when you're flustered, you used to do that all the time. Every Thanksgiving we would have 'roast beast' for dinner because you refused to admit you called it the wrong thing when you were twelve." His voice was quiet now, as if trying not to talk over the movie.

A long sigh escaped me. "I can't believe no one corrected me until I was *twenty* years old! That was the fault of all adults around me for letting that go on for so long. And seaman is a word, they're interchangeable."

I waited for him to bring up some other one-off time that I had improperly used a word, but after a beat he turned back to face the TV while I continued to work on his shoulder. Other than a few grunts and groans when I hit a sensitive spot, he remained quiet until I decided my work was done and relaxed next to him.

* * *

A week later, I woke up just like I had every morning– in my own bed. The only culprit for moving me from the couch to my bed every night was adamant in insisting I made my way to the bed on my own. Even the night that I pretended to sleep just to catch him carrying me to bed, the second my head hit the pillow I was out like a light.

My light pink comforter thrown on the opposite side of the bed, I swung to my feet to start my day. Thankfully it was the weekend, so I got a few extra hours of sleep. This game of cat and mouse with Ryan sleeping on the couch was messing up my bedtime.

In the kitchen, I found a note in scribbly handwriting that Ryan was at the gym, and to my utter dismay, I found the coffee pot already mostly full. Nothing like watery coffee to start my morning. I made my cup with Ryan's normal strength coffee and sat by my window to enjoy my few minutes of peace before my phone started ringing.

"Good morning," I sing-songed.

"Morning, I was just checking to make sure we were still on for baby shopping today?" Georgia asked.

I sat up straighter and my grip on my coffee became tight. I really needed to do a better job of putting stuff in my calendar, especially with Ryan throwing everything off balance. I kept losing track of where and what I was supposed to be doing. Setting my coffee down and beginning to pace, I tried to remember what time we were going to meet.

"Right! Of course, I was just getting ready." Clothes were flying over my shoulder as I spoke and looked through my closet for the perfect outfit. Georgia Mitchell– correction– Georgia *Reid,* was my best friend and closest confidante. And she was pregnant with her very first baby. And I had forgotten we were going shopping for her. Worst. Godmother. Ever.

Well, Georgia hadn't told me I was going to be a godmother, but come on. I'm a shoo-in.

"How about I pick you up in thirty? Char is coming too, right? I can pick her up on my way," I offered into the phone pinned between my cheek and shoulder.

"Okay sounds good, I'll see you then. I feel like we haven't spoken in forever, I can't wait to hear about this whole Ryan situation."

* * *

"I like the dress," Charlotte complimented. The floor of my closet was currently filled with a pile of clothes, but in the commotion I found the perfect baby shopping dress. It was light blue with a bird pattern that sort of resembled storks if you looked closely.

The scanner Georgia used to select which items she wanted to put on her baby shower registry beeped loudly. I took a peek at the tiny polka dot swaddles before turning back to Char.

"Thanks, so am I allowed to actually buy things today?" I

asked.

Georgia's nose scrunched, and her hand absentmindedly went to her stomach. "For the third time, no. We're just finding things for the registry, and you're throwing the party, so you don't need to buy anything else."

Like there was a chance in hell of that happening. I put my hand on the empty cart in front of her until she looked up at my face. "I am *so* getting this baby a million things, don't try to delude yourself into thinking anything else. This is the only baby I get to be involved with in the foreseeable future, so I'm going all out."

She snickered at my tone before pointing me out of her way to turn down another aisle.

"So, how's Ryan?" Charlotte asked. "Nick told me he's been staying at yours for the last couple of weeks."

Her words were innocent while the raise of her eyebrows and quirk of her lips were anything but. I knew they would fuss about me and Ryan, but he was just staying with me. We were just friends. That was how it had been for years and always would be.

"It's been a week at most, and yes he's staying with me for the time being." I tidied a stack of messy blankets on the shelf next to me. "I think he's just avoiding seeing his mom honestly."

Ryan's mom wasn't a bad person, but everyone knew they had a bit of a strained relationship. And also, what grown man enjoys living with his mother? It made sense that he would rather live with a friend, and being the closest friend without a significant other or kid, I was the first choice. At least that was the reasoning I came up with late at night when I couldn't fall back asleep.

"So you're just two single friends, staying together in a one

31

bedroom apartment," Charlotte reiterated. "Very casual."

"I would let any of our friends stay with me if they wanted, you're just reading into things."

Georgia and Charlotte shared a look I gave to other teachers when a kid came in during break hours to ask for extra credit on an assignment they never turned in. Changing the subject before they could ask more questions, I asked Char about her engagement party coming up soon.

* * *

My purse slammed down on the nearest counter the second I stepped inside of my apartment. Kicking my shoes off and sighing, I happily made my way further inside and went to collapse on my couch, but instead, I found Ryan sitting in my spot.

"Long day?" he asked.

"It was a good day, but yes, long. Shopping is exhausting." I plopped down next to him and put my feet up on my small coffee table.

Ryan shuffled around the coffee table until he was standing up and disappeared into the kitchen. He came back with a warm plate of pasta and offered it to me. "I wasn't sure if you guys ate or not, so I figured I'd bring you back some dinner."

My eyes widened, and I sat up to reach for it. "Thanks, this looks great."

"Do you wanna play Rummy?"

I nodded, and we both sank down to the floor to sit around the coffee table criss-cross applesauce. I placed my pasta on the table next to me and continued eating while Ryan grabbed a pack of cards from his gym bag and started dealing them out between the both of us.

"It's been a while since we've done this," I noted.

Cards used to be a staple of our friendship, it was how it all started really. We were neighbors growing up, but didn't officially meet until a summer camp in middle school. Ryan was always the kid that kept to himself, while I made sure I knew anyone and everyone. The first time I ever truly heard him speak more than a few words was sitting at a picnic table playing cards with him.

The game was called 'bullshit' or, as I liked to call it, 'peanut butter'. It had to be played in a group so, one day, when we needed another number, I shouted for Ryan to come over and the rest was history. By the end of the month-long camp, we were both the reigning champs and rarely lost to even the camp counselors.

"You haven't forgotten how to play have you?" he asked.

"Obviously not. Go ahead and get your excuses ready for when I beat you."

He smirked and finished straightening up the deck. I put down my fork to focus as we began playing the game. I set down a card, and then he did as well. It was a familiar rhythm that spoke to my heart.

My mind wandered back to earlier, to the look Charlotte and Georgia shared when I said Ryan was staying with me for the time being. "So why did you decide to stay in Rosewood for the entire off-season this time?"

His eyes raised from the cards to meet mine. "I needed a change for a bit. Am I bothering you by staying here?"

Always so blunt and honest. "No, I'm just curious. You visit, but you haven't stayed this long since you left."

He was quiet for a long while, I continued playing the game, but gave up hope I would get another answer out of him. A car alarm sounded off in the distance, and he sighed heavily before speaking.

"My manager thinks I can make Team USA," he started.

I interrupted before he could continue- "What? That's amazing!"

Leaning over the coffee table, I gave him the best long arm hug I could without messing up our cards. "Seriously, that's so exciting! Why haven't you told anyone?"

"It's not official yet, I still have tryouts." His voice did not sound like someone was excited to play in the Olympics.

"Well, that's still great! It would mean you could travel again, right?"

He nodded while looking intensely at the cards in front of him. "Yeah, it should be fun."

Ryan often did this thing where he said one thing and meant the exact opposite. It took me years to figure it out, but once I did, it only got easier over time to tell when he was lying. He always hated when I called him out on it, but never denied that I was right.

As I was debating questioning him further, he laid down his last card and declared his victory with a small smirk on his face. He was testing me, and I was totally falling for the trap.

"Why aren't you excited?" I pouted while throwing down my last few cards and picking up my plate of pasta.

He started reshuffling the deck while my eyes followed his hands. "I like competing for a prize."

His eyes flicked up to mine as if he just presented me with some secret riddle to uncover. After spending thirty seconds trying to read between the lines, I gave up and spoke slowly, "Well, the Olympics is the greatest competition in the world with arguably the best prize. What's the issue?"

"Right, it's global, probably going to be held in London. I'd be playing with people I most likely don't know, in front of people that don't know me, for a medal that doesn't really mean much," he grumbled at the table.

"Did Ashton hit you over the head too many times with a volleyball or something? It's the *Olympics*," I emphasized.

He laughed quietly before looking me directly in the eye again. "Yeah, hard to argue with that."

I squeezed my eyes shut quickly before putting my hands over his to stop him from reshuffling the deck again. "Can you explain? Because I'm not following you at all here."

"I love playing, and I love competing. But the last few years I look up in the stands to see complete strangers. My teammates are strangers most of the time, a lot of the time we don't even speak the same language. It was hard to communicate." I nodded as he paused to think. "I don't know, I guess I'm just not– invested."

"So you're... homesick?" I questioned.

He gave me a sad smile and nodded slightly. My heart hurt for him. Every time I imagined Ryan out in another country following his dreams, I pictured him happy– sure, Ryan never smiled much, but I at least hoped he was fulfilled on the inside. To know that he wasn't made me want to wrap him up in a hug and never let go.

So I did just that.

"Reese, I think your hair is getting in the food," he mumbled into my shoulder that was surely suffocating him.

I pulled away and sat back down on my side of the coffee table to find marinara sauce in my hair. He chuckled at me and offered a napkin. I wiped away a rogue tear first before trying to clean the chunk of pasta-sauced hair the best that I could.

"You missed your friends," I concluded. Ryan and I hadn't spoken about anything deeper than game wins or challenging kids that I worked with in years. I wanted to make sure I heard everything he was willing to share.

He nodded once again and then rolled his eyes. "Yeah, something like that. Ready for me to kick your ass again?"

And just like that, new cards were dealt, but we were back to the same game we always played.

Chapter 4

Ryan

"Remind me again why Nick thought it would be a celebration of love to barbecue Clay alive?" I muttered to Will. The log he was carrying thudded to the ground as he grunted and gave me a look. "Don't get me wrong– I'm all for it. Should be entertaining, I like the irony of him being a firefighter and all. But not exactly romantic, is it?"

The firefighter in question walked up behind us and tossed two more logs on the pile like they were made of air before turning back to go grab more. Will leaned down to start making a structure out of the wood we had already gathered.

"Look man, we were just getting to the point where it wasn't awkward for him and Reese to hang out in the group. Don't ruin it."

"It was awkward for them?" I blurted out.

"Obviously, why wouldn't it be?" Will answered. Reese wasn't capable of awkwardness. I couldn't imagine any social setting in which she would be uncomfortable, and to think that Clay put her in that made me dislike him even more.

I shrugged my shoulders and got back to work carrying

wood. On the next round, I carried two logs, and Clay made sure to take three on the trip after that. By the time Nick and Ashton arrived we were both at four logs a piece and out of breath.

Nick handed me a beer as I rolled the biggest log over to sit on it. "I was expecting us to all pitch in to make the fire, but it looks like the two of you already took care of it."

"Do either one of you have a ruler to get this over with? Otherwise, we're going to have a bonfire that could be seen from space in an hour," Will said.

Ashton snickered and put his arm on my shoulder to lean on me as he sat down. They could laugh all they fucking wanted. I didn't need a ruler to know that my dick was bigger than Clay's.

The firefighter huffed and sat down next to Will. Nick offered him a beer too before sitting down with the rest of us. Cool air lightly wrapped around me as I sat back and admired the shoreline. It wasn't quite sunset yet, but the harsh sun was in its slow descent back to the horizon.

"When are the girls going to get here?"

Nick stuck his beer in the sand before getting up to go grab whatever else they had brought in Ashton's truck. "Should be in less than an hour, Georgia took them to go get some cupcakes from a bakery outside of town," he said offhandedly.

"Come on, Summers. Help me grab the rest of this." As the youngest in our friend group by a few years, I was used to being their errand boy. A subtle smirk tipped up on Clay's face. I held up my middle finger behind my back and closely followed Nick.

At the truck, he shoved a few foldable chairs my way, and we each grabbed a handle on a much bigger cooler between us. "Congrats, by the way. Charlotte is way out of your league, dude."

He grinned over at me like a fool. "Yeah, I know."

"Reese told me about Team USA," he said quietly soon after. I couldn't help the groan that escaped me. I hadn't told her to *not* say anything, but I did secretly hope that she would keep it to herself.

I focused my attention on my black tennis shoes that sank in the sand with every step. "It's not a big deal, this is your day."

He snorted before laughing at me. "She said you were trying to be lowkey about it, I haven't told Ash yet. Figured you would want to do that yourself."

Ashton played for the US in the Olympics himself almost four years ago. He was one of the youngest to ever be on the team, and would likely still have an amazing pro career if he hadn't taken himself out of the sport. Even though we had more in common, I always felt closer to Nick out of the two brothers. Probably because we both knew what it was like to live in a shadow.

Now, I was the residential pro-athlete, and it seemed like that was the only thing I brought to the table these days. There was a reason I hadn't wanted to share the possibility of Team USA with everyone, and talking about nothing but volleyball for the next few months was exactly it. This time away was supposed to be a breath of fresh air.

An hour later, Charlotte ran and leaped up on Nick's back to greet him. "It looks so good! You all did great."

"Sorry we took a while, the two places we went to didn't have red velvet so we had to go to a third." A sheepish looking Georgia with a very round stomach held out a tray of cupcakes.

39

Ashton took them from her and gently set them down on an empty chair before giving her a sickeningly sweet kiss. I had the sudden urge to stick my finger in my mouth and pretend to gag like I was a kid in elementary school. My head turned to find Reese, but I didn't spot anyone else with them.

Charlotte took a seat near me and winced a little before saying, "She's having some kind of student emergency. But she should be here soon."

I nodded and forced my body to relax into the chair. This was going to be a long night.

Once the third story about saving some kind of animal from a traumatic event was over, I decided to get up and go for a walk along the water. There were only so many cats in trees that I could take in a day. My beer was no longer cold, but I took a swig of it anyway.

"Wait up, Summers." I heard the call from a distance.

My pace slowed, but I didn't stop walking. The sun had set, so the bonfire and moonlight were the only two things illuminating my path. Clay's hand rested on my shoulder as he caught up with me.

Long ago, he was my team captain. We had never seen eye to eye. He was always too serious about things that didn't matter, and I had a bit of an issue with authority. Not to mention, a few years back I got a call that he was dating Reese. Asshole.

"Can we talk, or do you want to settle this by swimming in that freezing water and seeing who drowns first?" he asked.

"Be my guest," I mumbled around my beer bottle.

"Look, Reese and I ended things a long time ago. We weren't right for each other, so there's no competition there." He paused. I had no fucking clue how he wanted me to respond to that. "And for the record, I think you two would be great for each other."

I snorted. "Jumping on the 'Reese and Ryan are in love' bandwagon are you?" The laugh that escaped me sounded colder than I intended it to. "We're just friends."

"I heard you were staying with her." To his merit, Clay looked a little remorseful at the suggestion.

"Yes, I'm staying with her. As friends. It's been over a decade of us being nothing but friends, so I don't know when you're all going to get it in your head."

He nodded, and for a moment I thought he would let me finish my walk in peace. Suddenly, his shoulder jutted out, and he body checked me into stumbling in the ice cold water. I righted myself and turned to face him, furious as hell. His biceps might be as thick as tree trunks, but I had height and length on him. I liked my odds in a fight.

His stance held no hostility, though. If anything, his face looked a bit sad. "Stop bullshitting me, you've never been good at lying."

I reached out to shove him a little anyway, still feeling like I had a justification to start throwing punches. That water clung to my skin like thousands of stabbing needles.

"I'm not bullshitting you. Reese Finch and I would never work. She practically never leaves Rosewood, nearly everyone in this damn town relies on her to help them out in some way." My voice lowered to a growl. "I travel the world for a living and never think about anyone but my damn self. We would never even see each other."

By the time I finished speaking, I was standing much closer to him than I remembered. He took a step back and opened his mouth, most likely to tell me off.

"Hey, guys!" Reese's cheery voice broke through the tense air like a bell. "Sorry I'm late. Charlotte told me you two decided to check out the water. It's most definitely freezing, so I hope you're not thinking about taking a swim."

Her smile fell a little when she took in our posture and the frustration on our faces. I backed up a bit, and relaxed my hand until it was no longer balled up in a fist.

"Is everything okay?" Now she was glancing back and forth between us like a tennis match was going on.

Clay chuckled and wrapped his arm around my shoulders. "Yeah, we're all good. Summers just had a little too much to drink is all." He squeezed my arm. "Right, buddy?"

The word 'buddy' lit up my urge to smack the fuck out of him all over again. But Reese was standing in front of me in a short red dress and she had some sort of pretty earrings on— were those cherries? So I blew out a breath and nodded in agreement with Clay.

Reese's dimples returned, and she positioned herself on the opposite side of me as Clay. She picked up my left arm and wrapped it around her shoulders before dragging me back to the bonfire, where a crowd of people that I knew well long ago now felt a little too much like strangers.

"What took you so long?" The question came out a lot whinier than I intended.

"Seems like you were having plenty of fun without me," she teased.

I leaned onto her a little more than I needed to and made a grunt of disagreement. "Your friends suck."

Her warm hand made its way to my ear and she pulled at it to scold me with a grin. "They're your friends, too. You were just complaining the other night about how you missed them."

The caveman trailing behind us laughed into his hand. I

flipped him the bird behind Reese's back before tilting my head to speak quietly into her ear. "That was confessed in the comfort of our home. You just broke my trust, Finch."

Her cheeks pinkened, and she stayed silent before whispering back to me while keeping her eyes set on the bonfire. "I wasn't aware it was *our* home."

We made our way back to the crowd and were welcomed with a symphony of loud voices. My seat was the only one left, so I collapsed into the foldable chair and gestured for Reese's elbow.

"Sit. We're going to be here all night, your little boyfriend has only gotten through three of his thirteen cat-saving stories."

"We broke up *years* ago, you jerk."

Reese jokingly yanked her arm away from me before pouting and sitting down sideways across my knees. She perched there like an awkward little bird. Instead of staring at her, I wrapped my arm around her waist and pulled her closer to lean against my chest.

The guys and Charlotte were in the middle of a heated debate about whether or not football was interesting when I noticed Reese shivering. Her bare arms were covered in goosebumps. Sighing to myself, I sat up to pull off my sweatshirt and started pulling it over her head.

Wordlessly, she accepted the warm clothing and helped me pull her arms through. I left the hood up since she looked adorable surrounded in the fabric. The ocean breeze pulled a few strands of her hair loose, and when she turned to me, I brushed away a piece of hair that was stuck to her glossy lips.

"Thanks," she whispered. I watched her eyelashes flutter in the light of the bonfire.

Her look kept me warm despite the cool night air. "Do you

want me to move us closer to the fire?"

Without waiting for her response, I lifted her from my lap. I stood in the sand with her clinging onto my neck as I held her up. Instead of putting her feet down so she could stand, I moved our chair closer to the fire with my foot before sitting back down with Reese still in my lap.

I caught a few glances our way, but decided to ignore them in favor of witnessing one of my favorite sights. Reese was stumbling her way through finding a word to start off what was sure to be a severe scolding on my end.

Her mouth closed and opened a couple more times before she found her footing. "I could have just stood up! I'm capable of standing Ryan, you didn't need to carry me."

I leaned forward into the side of her head and rested my forehead on my hoodie that covered her cheek to hide my smile. Her voice raised into a high-pitched whine anytime I did anything for her.

When she noticed my chest shaking from silent laughter, she fully turned in my lap to be face to face. "I'm serious, Ryan. You need to learn to use your words, you're an untrained dog who was taught to hit a ball for a living."

My face rose to meet hers and she softened at the sight of me laughing. Hand over my heart I swore, "It won't happen again. You have my deepest apologies for lifting you without warning." My other hand was resting on her lower back with two fingers distinctly crossed.

She sighed and pointedly turned to face away from me, striking up a conversation with Georgia who sat to the right of us. I was given the silent treatment for the next half hour until everyone decided it was time to start packing up.

Of course, of all the cars to ride home in, Clay managed to

make his way into Reese's Toyota. A very tipsy Charlotte and Nick laughed together in the backseat while I rushed to strap in my seatbelt. At least I had the foresight to call shotgun.

"Couldn't he have ridden with Georgia and Ashton?" I loudly whispered to Reese while leaning over the middle console.

Clay let out a loud sigh before I heard the car door behind me slam shut. To my side I found a very heated glare from Reese.

"His house isn't far from us. Now shut up and drink this." A lukewarm bottle of water was dropped in my lap. I saluted her and took a large gulp while she rolled her eyes and tried her best to hold her grumpy face. It lasted about ten seconds.

The stars shone bright in the night sky, and the salty air whipped my hair out of my face through the cracked window. I looked back at Reese to watch her smile slowly return.

Charlotte slapped her hand on my headrest and leaned forward from her middle seat. "I can't believe all of this is happening at the same time," she exclaimed with a bigger smile on her face than I had ever seen.

She turned to Nick and continued, "We're getting married." He reached for her free hand and kissed it sweetly. I looked away and wished I drank a couple more beers. "Georgia and Ashton are having a baby. Another baby. Ruth is getting a sister, I mean."

Her rambling continued, and her hand reached forward to grab Reese's arm. "And you and Ryan are together!" Nick grabbed his fiance's hand and gently pushed her to sit back against the seat. Realizing her fumble, Charlotte corrected herself, "staying together, I mean. I'm just so happy."

Nick chuckled awkwardly. "Sorry, she gets really chatty when she's drunk."

45

Reese and I shared a knowing look. The comments about us getting together one day started back when we were fifteen, and showed no signs of stopping anytime soon. It would take a big shiny rock on her finger and some loser's name engraved on it for people to get it through their heads. I cringed at the thought.

When we reached Nick's diner, I got out to help him get Charlotte up the stairs to their loft on the second floor. He was nearly as unstable as she was. I made sure they both ended up in bed before returning to the car. Clay and Reese stopped speaking the second I opened the door.

I got in and stayed quiet until our next stop, where Clay thanked Reese for the ride and was on his merry way. We sat in his driveway for a few minutes when Reese turned to me.

"Why do you feel the need to be so rude to him? He's our friend," she asked. Well, for one, he had a very punchable face. Two, he dated my best friend without even consulting me when I was halfway across the world and–

"I dunno, there's just something about him," I said to the window.

She stared at me while I avoided eye contact for a few beats longer. "He literally helps others for a living, Ryan. What's not to like?"

"And he'll be sure to never let us forget it, can we stop for some ice cream?" Desserts always distracted her.

Her laugh was quiet. "The cat stories do get old after a while." She moved to put the car in reverse before craning her neck to see behind us.

I nearly had whiplash from how fast I turned to her. Her laugh got louder at the incredulous look on my face. "It's true," she defended. "I've heard the one about the cat stuck in the

46

sewer at least twenty times."

The smirk on my face grew even wider. I never thought I would see Reese Finch talking shit about someone, much less a guy she dated. And I was loving every second of it.

I propped my elbow up on the arm rest between us and lowered my chin to lean on my hand, listening intently. The cocky grin I was surely wearing felt unfamiliar, but good. "Please, go on," I insisted.

Chapter 5

Reese

Carrying the weight of a six foot something professional athlete was not easy. And I swore Ryan was leaning on me more than he needed to. We managed to make it to the rickety elevator of my apartment building when I took his arm off of my shoulders and let him lean on the wall.

"How exactly did you go from stable enough to help Char and Nick up the stairs, to now being completely incapable of walking on your own?" I chided while catching my breath.

He let out a quiet laugh. He was awfully giggly today. The elevator beeped, and we exited on my floor. This time, I made no offer to assist him down the hallway, and he walked in a perfectly straight line down the awful striped carpeted hall.

Once we were inside, I began our favorite argument. Maybe since he was more relaxed than usual, he would finally give in. "You should take the bed tonight," I offered.

Not once had he slept in my bed in the few weeks that he stayed here. He insisted on torturing himself by sleeping on my small, stiff sofa. And even on the nights I refused to give in, he stayed awake until I fell asleep and moved me to my bed.

He was silent while we took off our shoes, and I shrugged off the sweatshirt he let me borrow. It wasn't until I reached the doorway of my bedroom to get ready for bed that he spoke.

"What if we shared it?"

I stood in place. "Shared what?"

Refusing to answer my dumb question, he stared at me blankly while my mind raced. "We can't share my bed, you're too big," I decided.

He took a step closer, and in one stride was halfway across my living room.

"If I can fit on that thing," Ryan lazily tilted his head to point at the sofa. "Then I think I'm capable of sharing your bed."

I looked down at my mismatched socks to hide my smile. The mental image of him curling up on my couch like a cat always made me laugh. Hair fell in my face as I lowered my head, and he reached forward to tuck it behind my ear.

My eyes raised to meet his when I spoke, "We could get you one of those boxes contortionists fit in. Seems like you have untapped potential."

The hand that lingered on my face reached back to gently tug at my braid. His mouth remained in a flat line, but his eyes squinted playfully.

"Or I could just go sleep outside with the cats. I'd be in better company," he snarked.

I backed up into my room to start taking off my jewelry. He followed and sat on my bed, making sure to lean back and stretch out until his limbs nearly reached all four edges of the bed. I caught his eye in the mirror and scoffed.

"I hear they serve a complimentary breakfast with your stay there. You'd be better fed, too."

He yawned to hide a smirk. "I'm not really a fan of kibble,

49

but thanks."

The clasp on my necklace cut into my thumb on the fourth try unhooking it. I cringed and looked at it closely before determining I wasn't bleeding. A tap on my hip made my gaze fall to the mirror where I saw Ryan sitting up on the corner of the bed behind me, gesturing for me to back up so he could take off the necklace for me.

"I can do it," I assured.

"I know, but let me," he insisted.

Tired from a long day, I decided to give in. I took a couple of steps back to be within his reach when he gently pulled me closer to sit on his thigh.

"I'm tall, but not that tall, Reese," he said softly.

I felt slightly out of breath when his hand brushed against the nape of my neck to move my hair further out of his way. It felt like he took minutes to unhook the clasp, and I wasn't sure if that was because he was struggling or my sense of time was thrown off by his closeness.

When he was done, he opened my right hand and pressed the necklace into it. My heart slowed as I stood up and returned it to its rightful place on my dresser. Feeling more confident with the distance between us, I made eye contact again to find his eyes already on me.

"You're blushing," he stated. His face gave away no amusement, but I could hear the teasing in his voice.

Sure, my knees felt a little wobbly, and yes, my face felt hot, but I would never admit to *blushing* over my best friend. This was nothing more than a side effect of not having physical intimacy with another human in so long. My mind was reeling at the simple act of his hand brushing against my neck. How embarrassing.

I fixated my glare at his reflection in the mirror before declaring, "I am not. It's just hot in here."

He stood up behind me and put a finger under my chin, so I was staring directly at the mirror in front of us. "I know I'm slightly color blind, but that looks pink to me."

My eyes followed his hand as it cupped my chin to trail his pointer finger across my freckle covered cheek. He was right, it was definitely flushed and only continued to darken as he waited for my response.

This felt different from how Ryan usually teased me. The look on his face made me take pause in calling out his own actions. Our banter always felt more like a dance back and forth, but this moment had the heaviness of deciding whether or not we would jump off a cliff together.

Before I had time to straighten out my face and thoughts, Ryan stepped away again and started walking around my room. Not that there was much room to explore, the only available floor space was a U-shape around my bed that led to either my bathroom, closet, or the hall. His pacing stopped in front of a collage board filled with old pictures from before I went to college.

I took the opportunity to flee to my bathroom while he was distracted and wash my face with ice cold water. *Was Ryan Summers flirting with me?* No. I'm not his type. Not to mention the fact that we had been friends for years with no other indicators he was interested. Maybe he was just acting differently because he got a little tipsy.

Reaching for my face towel blindly, I patted my damp face before going for my toothbrush when I noticed a figure looming behind me. A gasp escaped me out of habit before I clutched my nonexistent pearls.

51

"Easy, scaredy cat," Ryan cooed. "I just thought we could save time, and the door was open."

He reached for his navy blue toothbrush next to my bright orange one that I had almost knocked over. He squeezed toothpaste for himself before gesturing that I should hold out my toothbrush for him to cover as well. Minty white toothpaste spilled over the sides before I wet it and started brushing next to him.

I had never felt so scrutinized doing such a mundane task before. The sounds of bristles on teeth filled my ears while I pointedly looked at every object in my bathroom other than Ryan. The bright peachy pattern of my shower curtain had caught my eye for too long when he nudged me with his elbow.

Stepping to the side to give him room, I turned my back to him while he spit into the sink and rinsed out his mouth. I continued brushing while he waited, and I guessed I took longer than usual, because I found him looking at the clock amusedly when I turned back around.

After taking the time to brush out my hair slowly, I decided to join Ryan back in my room where I found him on my bed. He had my paperback copy of *The Outsiders* folded in his hand while he skimmed through the pages.

His face tipped up to acknowledge me. "Ready for bed?"

I nodded slowly and sat on the side closest to the bathroom door and furthest away from him. He pointedly stared at the large space between us, and then at my legs nearly falling off the side of the bed.

He placed the book back where he found it on my pile atop my bookshelf before getting up and walking into the living room. I thought he had forgotten something and waited dumbly for him to come back.

When I saw him walking past the door with pillows and a blanket, I got up to trail behind him into the living room. "What are you doing?" I asked.

"I'll sleep out here, you go sleep in there," he said firmly. No anger, no passive aggressiveness, just the assured stubbornness of Ryan Summers.

"Why? I thought you wanted to share my bed." I grabbed the spare pillow to bring it into my room for him.

He looked down at me through his messy hair. "You're uncomfortable, I'll just sleep out here."

"I'm not uncomfortable sleeping next to you," I argued.

"Your body language says otherwise. You won't hurt my feelings Reese, you could have just told me." He sat and waited for me to give him his pillow back.

Instead of obliging him like I usually did, I reached down to rip the blanket off of the couch next to him before marching into my room. "I'm not uncomfortable," I declared loudly, so he could hear me from the other room.

He appeared in the doorway again, watching me put his pillow next to mine and pull back the covers to make a spot for myself to slip under. I sat down and made myself comfortable before crossing my arms and silently challenging him to a staring match. He heaved out a breath that somewhat resembled a laugh before bowing his head and joining me on the bed.

He pulled back the blankets to his side and slid in next to me. This shouldn't be anything new, we had been sleeping under the same roof for weeks now, and we had plenty of sleepovers in high school. Although then, he'd slept on the floor. I figured his back wasn't built for that anymore though.

"It's been a while since I slept next to someone. I'm nervous, that's all," I admitted.

He settled his focus on me. Those brown eyes glittered in the faint light from my stained glass floor lamp. "Worried I'll snore? I make no promises I won't, but you can just kick me if I'm bothering you."

"No," I spoke without thinking. My brow furrowed, and I laid flat on my back to think deeply before responding thoughtfully. "I like having you here."

"Really?" His question was genuine, eager almost.

I turned to him and nodded. "Of course I do. Every time you come back to visit now, I feel like I get to experience a new version of you. This time, you're much more open than you've ever been before."

Which was true, what I made sure to leave out was that sometimes it felt like with each visit home he felt a little further away from me. Except now. This visit, I was perfectly aware of how *close* he was to me. Literally and figuratively, as proven by his bicep pushing against mine as he laid down to face the ceiling.

"Do you think Nick and Charlotte will work out?" he asked.

My neck craned as I yanked my head over to look at him. "What on Earth do you mean? Of course I do, they're getting married."

"Marriages don't always work out." He pushed his hand furthest from me behind his head and into his hair. "I'm pretty sure the divorce rate is like sixty percent now or something."

I stared at him, completely dumbfounded. "Nick and Charlotte aren't just numbers on a chart, they're our friends. I know they'll work out. They're happy as can be."

He sighed and continued looking at my popcorn ceiling. I looked back to it as well to try to see what pattern he was staring at so I could follow his train of thought. Maybe there was a hidden message up there I was missing. I came up with nothing.

"Why would you ask that? Do you not think they're good together?" I questioned.

"They seem perfect, they've known each other since high school. Nick has had a crush on her since then, they both had time to experience life outside of each other, and still chose one another. Seems perfect," he said quietly.

"They'll work out. You're too much of a pessimist sometimes," I scolded.

I blinked at the ceiling again. Those white popcorn kernels weren't being any more helpful in explaining than Ryan was. We sat in silence for a few minutes longer, the warmth I felt from his side of the bed was nice. I tried to remember the last time I felt comfortable in silence with someone like this.

"Do you remember our marriage contract in high school?" I asked with a smile on my face.

He scoffed. "Your time is running out. You've only got two years and three months left until we get hitched."

I propped myself up on my elbows and faced him with a laugh. "You do remember!" I exclaimed while smiling. "I wasn't aware you were counting down the days, I'm pretty sure I still have it somewhere at my mom's house."

He playfully rolled his eyes and pushed back his hair. "I bet. That must be why you dated Clay for years, buying time until our contract was due."

Grabbing at his shirt, I tried my best to intimidate him with a smile finding its way to my face. "Take. It. Back."

He laughed at my demand and flipped us over, so I was now on my back, and he was the one looming over me. "Never.

Admit it, you've been planning our wedding this whole time."

His hand under my lower back raised the hairs on the nape of my neck. He was so close, our noses nearly touching.

"You're jealous. If you need to lie a little to boost your ego, I get it, Ryan. You're having a hard time finding a woman who will date you, but I won't judge. You can't be good at everything," I proclaimed dramatically.

A completely false statement. Ryan *was* good at everything. One of those people that can pick up something on the first try and do it effortlessly. But I couldn't let him think he's some hero I've been pining over all these years, because it wasn't true. Sometimes he needed humbling.

He glanced down at my gloating smile and mirrored it with his own. My breathing hitched as I really took in the sight in front of me. His nose barely brushed against mine as I watched his smile fade into a flat line. I studied every inch of his face, not because I didn't already know it, but because it was rare to see him so open like this. It was like reading my favorite book from an entirely new perspective.

"Reese," he murmured. His arm that wasn't wrapped around my back lifted up, so he could cup my face with his hand. His thumb brushed across my cheek, and I thought I could see him counting my freckles.

I had no words. My heart was beating out of my chest, and I was sure he would tease me for it. He never did.

Instead, he leaned in to nudge his nose against mine. I gripped onto his shirt for dear life, as if this was a dream, and it could be ripped away from me at any second. I stopped breathing to make sure it actually was real, but before I could determine how long I held my breath for, his lips pushed against mine.

56

It was slow, gentle, and sweet. Everything I knew Ryan wasn't, and it made my head spin. This wasn't a heat of the moment kiss, this was a *holy shit I have feelings for you* kind of kiss.

After my brain was thoroughly melted, he leaned back slightly, so we were separated. We were still close enough that I could feel his hair brushing against my forehead and his legs press against mine as he held up the bulk of his weight to hover over me.

His eyes locked with mine, and he waited. For a full minute my mind was reeling with hundreds of questions. Why is he kissing me? If he just wanted to sleep with someone, he could go find countless other women, and why now? Did he even want to sleep with me? Was this some kind of test?

What came out of my mouth wasn't a question at all, though. "We shouldn't do this."

Ryan laughed dryly, as if he expected me to say this. He sounded relieved if anything, his crooked smirk returned with his smile, and he nudged my nose again.

"Do you want to do this?" he asked, his gaze flickering down to my mouth. I realized I was biting my lip and forced my teeth to release it.

Obviously. If just one kiss was any indicator, I absolutely wanted everything he was offering and more. But he was my best friend, this would complicate everything from here on out. What if we can't be friends after this? What if-

"Reese," he murmured. He sounded like he was praying to someone, me, I hoped. "Stop thinking about everyone else, it's simple. Do *you* want to do this?"

It was never that simple. But maybe it could be. Just this once.

"Yes," I huffed confidently.

His hand pushed up into my hair to rest on the back of my neck. His thumb wrapped around to brush my jaw comfortingly. He messily trailed kisses from where my jaw met my ear on the other side of my face down to the base of my neck. Goosebumps raised everywhere his lips touched, I had never been more turned on in my life.

Usually this was where I would end it. No strings attached sex wasn't my thing, and once I knew someone well enough to decide to sleep with them, I had a bad habit of immediately getting attached. I wasn't capable of just having sex and enjoying myself, I always felt like I owed them something after.

Maybe just this once, I could have fun. Ryan was my best friend, I trusted him to not take advantage of me after and string me along. Sure, it might complicate our friendship, but we both would never risk messing that up. And it had been so long since I had done anything for me.

"Do you want me to stop?" he asked again.

I shook my head hurriedly. I wanted him to go faster, he was being far too patient and controlled when my heart was racing like I was running a marathon.

He placed a sweet kiss on my cheek. "Words, Reese." At least he sounded out of breath now, too. The breathiness in his voice caught me by surprise, and when I studied his eyes, I found the same level of hungriness I was sure reflected in mine.

"Don't stop," I muttered, greedily reaching for the back of his shirt to yank it up and over his head.

Chapter 6

Ryan

Waking up and not knowing what bed I was laying in ranked in my least favorite feelings. It happened often, cold, scratchy duvet covers of hotels were never a pleasant way to wake up. Once, in Germany, I had even slammed my face into the wall. I busted open my nose because I thought I was in a different beigey hotel room and forgot the bed was pressed against the wall when I tried to stumble to the bathroom in the morning.

The one exception was the feeling of waking up in Reese's bed. I didn't even need to look around, I smelled her fruity orange cinnamon shampoo the second I woke up. Her limbs draped over me were a comforting weight. I kept my eyes closed for a while, in case it was actually a dream. They didn't open until I felt her shifting against me.

I reveled in the feeling long enough. My patience wore out, and I looked to my left to find the prettiest sight I had ever seen. Filtered light streamed in through blinds and landed across Reese's cheek. The morning sun must have bothered her because her arm was raised over her forehead, but she was still in a deep sleep.

Curly hair was splayed out over her pillow, and her perfectly shaped mouth was slightly open. The shape of her cupid's bow deserved to be displayed in museums. I watched her huffing out each breath for quite some time. It wasn't often you got to see Reese Finch so relaxed, so I was going to take advantage of every second.

Her leg that was pressed against mine rolled away from me, and I realized I should probably get up. Last night was fucking amazing, everything I could have hoped for and more, but I had no idea how Reese would react this morning. Doing anything without a twelve step plan beforehand wasn't her thing, so she probably needed a minute alone to process.

I slowly sat up and shifted the blankets over to replace my warmth against Reese's side. I found my shirt at the foot of the bed. As I was leaning down to look underneath the bed to find my boxers, I heard a loud thump.

I shot up to find Reese's spot empty. Shrugging on my shirt, I spotted my boxers and yanked them on as well before walking around to find Reese sitting on the floor. Sheets were tangled around her and she hurriedly pulled them up to her neck to cover herself.

"You okay?" I asked carefully.

She nodded, her eyes as big as an owl's. I sighed and leaned down to crouch on the floor in front of her. "I know I made you cum twice, but are your legs really not working?"

When it was clear my joke didn't land, I took a different approach. "What's wrong, baby?"

Her eyes widened even larger somehow at the pet name, and she pushed herself up to sit on the bed. "We slept together!" She whispered like her mother was in the next room and could hear us.

60

I rubbed at the crease between my eyebrows and lowered my voice. "We did."

"We're friends, we can't sleep together! I'm sorry, I've never done anything so impulsive," she whisper-yelled.

"Why exactly are we whispering?" I asked.

"I don't think I can even look you in the eye," she said into her lap. "What about our friendship? We've been friends for so long, I trust you more than I trust anyone. I don't want to risk losing that."

My heart dropped out into my stomach, and I felt my face hardening into my normal guarded look. She regretted it. I knew going too fast wasn't the best idea with her, but I never expected her to regret it. She only saw me as a friend, nothing more. It was all of my worst fears confirmed in one swift blow.

My attempts to lighten the mood continued to fail, so I offered the only logical solution to her panic, "Then we won't do it again."

That seemed to put her at ease, her hands stopped clutching at the sheets so desperately, and her shoulders rolled down to their normal height. She took some deep breaths, I assumed in some sort of breathing technique, before leaning back against her headboard.

"Right," she said, still exasperated, but calmer than before. "Just a one time thing. We've been friends for like a decade, it shouldn't be an issue right?"

She looked to me for confirmation. I nodded. If she needed me to be her friend, then that's what we would be. BFFs forever.

I collected her pajamas to give back to her. "Mind if I take a shower?"

She shook her head, and I retreated to her small bathroom.

I stopped the door just as it was about to close. "By the way, did you know you talk in your sleep?"

"What?" she gasped. "What did I say?"

"Those are secrets that I will take to my grave, Finch. I must say, your opinions on social media influencers are pretty scandalous. Be out in a few."

Messing with her was always my favorite pastime. If she wanted to stay friends, I would do everything in my power to make sure we stayed close. One night wouldn't ruin my relationship with Reese, we had years and years to fall back on.

I pulled the shower head as high as possible, so I wouldn't have to duck too much to fit under it. This time I didn't even bother trying to make it hot, I felt every sharp needle of the freezing cold water to distract me from the disaster that was playing out in front of me.

* * *

The most awkward morning of my life came to a peak when I told Reese I would find somewhere else to stay. Her face looked surprised, although she hadn't spoken to me all morning. I wanted to spend time with her, that's why I was here in the first place, but not at the expense of her happiness.

"You don't have to leave," she said.

I couldn't help but chuckle. "I know, but I think it's best."

"I want you to stay," she argued. "I'm sorry, I'm just not used to this." Her arm waved between us, and her cheeks heated to a rosy pink, just like they had every time she looked at me today.

I nodded. If she was too nice to kick me out, I would do it

myself. "I can't keep sleeping on that couch, and we've proven sleeping on the bed together isn't the best idea. It's not a big deal, I can probably stay with Charlotte and Nick for a few days before I find somewhere."

Her eyebrows shot up. "You want to stay with two soon-to-be newlyweds?"

She had a point. "It's just temporary," I deadpanned.

Reese pulled her lip between her teeth in the way that always drove me crazy. She stayed quiet for a minute before solving all of our problems, just like she always did.

"I know," she chirped happily. "What if we get a futon? I've clearly needed a new couch for a while, it's a win win."

I sighed. "Are you just doing this to make me happy, or do you really want me to stay?"

If she needed a new couch, I would buy it and be on my way. I'd already offered to buy her a new one several times since being here. She never seemed interested in my offer until now.

"Of course I want you here, we're still friends. Right?" The uncertainty in her face nearly killed me.

"We'll always be friends, Reese, don't be stupid," I scoffed.

Her cute smile returned to her face. "Okay, a futon then."

Her suggestion that my leaving would solidify the fact that us sleeping together changed our friendship, made my decision easy. I nodded in agreement. "Let's go buy a futon."

Chapter 7

Reese

Living with Ryan after having a scandalous one night stand proved to be a fun new challenge. Every time he got out of the shower shirtless with his damp hair flopping in every direction, I did my best to focus on anything else in the room. Even when he was fully clothed, I couldn't stop myself from staring. It wasn't hard to imagine them off now that I was very familiar with what he looked like without them.

I felt like such a loser. The one time I went against my better judgment, and I slept with Ryan of all people. When he was literally living with me. The worst part of it all was the paper thin walls and general closeness of my apartment, the only time I was able to blow off some steam was in the shower, and even then it felt risky.

The first few weeks were spent with slightly awkward eye contact and me overthinking every single touch. We stood in the kitchen one day, making dinner together and his pinky brushed against mine when he reached over for the spoon I was holding. I was up thinking about that for hours.

It was undeniable, Ryan Summers was the best lay I had ever

had. Even men I'd been with for years didn't pick up on what I enjoyed in bed like he had in a few hours. There was no self consciousness and overthinking about what I looked like. I was completely in the moment. And that moment was hot as hell.

Thankfully, I had work to keep me busy. We were preparing a play for the theater club. Between sewing costumes, making props, and practices, all my free time was spent. The rest of the waking hours I had were easily filled with my regular tenth grade english classes and extra tutoring I did.

About a month and a half had passed since The Incident, as I called it in my head, and we found ourselves in a familiar situation. Ryan squirmed in his spot on my bed for the hundredth time, and I couldn't help but laugh at his childishness. I leaned back to let him take a breath while I pulled back my hair since it was getting in my face.

Once he was patiently waiting for me to continue, I got back to work. Only for him to once again start squirming in his seat.

"Can you just stop moving please?!" I said, exasperated.

He huffed out an annoyed breath. "I'm trying. It's cold and tickles."

The slight downturn of his lips made him look even more ridiculous. Half of his face was covered in black and gray face paint. I told him he could either come up with a Halloween costume or I would make one for him. He must have underestimated me, because he seemed to be regretting his life decisions up to this point as I put the paint brush back to his nose.

I stood and walked back a few feet to admire my work from a distance. He certainly looked skeleton-like. I was no artist, but it was hard to mess up a few circles around the eyes and triangle for the nose. My pink headband that I use to push back my hair when I wash my face was placed daintily on his head to pull the longer pieces of his hair back enough so I could paint his forehead.

My smile grew wider as I took in his annoyed expression with the paint and headband, and I couldn't help but laugh. He sighed and stood up to go to the bathroom to see for himself. Pulling the headband off his head, he did a few turns to see all the angles of my work. Then he looked in the mirror to find me smiling behind him.

"I look ridiculous," he pouted.

"You look great, don't be silly," I smiled and patted him on the back.

"Everyone is going to point and laugh."

"You *are* young enough to still trick or treat, if you want, I'm sure I can drop you off at a neighborhood to go get some candy."

His arm wrapped around my middle to pull me closer and grumble in my ear, "It's a two year difference, Reese."

I pulled out of his arms to laugh at his pout. "You started this. If I'm ancient, you're definitely an iPad kid."

He reached up to pinch my cheek lightly and indiscreetly tucked his phone that was always in hand, in his pocket. "Where's your face paint?"

"My costume does enough of the work, I don't need it," I said with a gloating smile. My slight nerves about tonight kicked back in. "We still aren't telling anyone about us sleeping together, right?"

"Do you want people to know?"

"Not really. I just don't want them to make a big deal out

of it." That was an understatement. If our friends knew we'd finally slept together, we would never hear the end of it. "I mean you saw what it was like with Clay, not that it's the same situation, but I just don't want our friend group to be different. I like things the way they are."

His eyelids lowered as he looked down at me over his nose. "Then we don't need to tell them."

* * *

We walked into the house filled with people dressed in half assed costumes and red cups in their hands. Music flowed throughout the house, and I grabbed Ryan's hand as I marched through hallways and rooms to get us both drinks.

I spotted Georgia through a doorway and waved at her happily before dragging Ryan back toward her. In the sunroom, we found a pool table surrounded by our friends. It looked like Ashton, Charlotte, and Nick were playing while Will stood in a corner giving quiet corrections. I gave him a small smile of acknowledgement before wrapping my arms around Georgia's shoulders.

"You look great!" I said over the music. She was dressed in a poofy pink dress and tiara.

I watched her look around frantically for something. "I don't know where I put my wand, but it's here somewhere. People keep asking if I'm a fairy, so I guess they somewhat get the idea."

We agreed a few weeks ago to dress up as Glinda and Elphaba from Wicked, almost entirely from my pleading with her. Georgia was the only one who somewhat understood my obsession with the Broadway musical.

Ryan stepped forward to give Georgia a one-armed hug quickly. "Woah, I didn't expect you to dress up! You both look great," she added.

"See, no one's pointing and laughing," I teased while nudging Ryan with my elbow.

"Reese's idea," he mumbled in return. Her smile only widened, and he gave some grumbled excuse before turning his attention to the pool table and greeting the others.

"You two seem to be getting along," she whispered as soon as he was out of earshot.

My head tilted. "What do you mean?"

Georgia rolled her eyes playfully and took a drink from her water bottle. "You were holding hands, it just seems like you two are getting cozy." I gave her a look. "Don't get all defensive, it's just an observation!"

"I was just making sure he was following," I said, toootally not in a defensive way.

This was the first time we had hung out with all of our friends in a group since we slept together. Sixty seconds in, and we were already getting comments. This was the very reason we decided not to tell anyone, since I could only imagine the amount of 'I told you so's' we would get. Our plan of acting normal would work, though. I was sure they wouldn't be able to tell any difference.

Hands slipped around my waist and tugged me sideways into a hug. I turned to find Charlotte, in her usual plain black jeans with a white knitted sweater. She wasn't usually touchy feely, so I had an inkling she'd had a few drinks already.

"You're not dressed up," I accused.

She pulled out of the hug to answer, "You know that's not my thing."

68

"You're no fun!" I said playfully. "I could have brought you so many costumes, I had too many ideas this year."

She laughed and pointed at Nick. "If it makes you feel better, I did have cat ears, but he stole them."

I looked over to find her dark haired fiance at the pool table cueing up with a set of black cat ears on his head. At least someone in the room, other than Georgia and I, was in the spirit. It was pitiful, but it was something.

We spent most of the night out there in that room. Although, we did have the occasional guests join for a game or two. I never even saw the owner of the house, who was an old friend from high school and my current dentist. I was happy to just let my friends commandeer the pool table and hang out with them. There was even a comfy couch in the corner where Georgia and I sat after being completely embarrassed by our pool skills.

"Come on, Reese, we'll play together," Ryan called from across the room.

I looked at him through my lashes as he walked toward me. "What good is playing together going to do? Apparently, I'm the worst pool player in history," I declared dramatically while looking at my nails to seem uninterested.

He gave me one of his rare smiles. "Well, at least we know you can't get any worse." He laughed at the sight of my jaw on the floor. "Come on, I'll help you."

Ryan and Will set up for a new game together while I waited patiently. I suddenly had the feeling everyone was staring at me, and it only got worse when Ryan handed me the cue stick. He stood behind me while I did my best to line up the shot.

"You're holding it wrong, here." Suddenly, I felt his very warm chest against my back as he leaned over and wrapped his arms around mine. His hand moved my fingers to the right position, and all I could focus on was the heat of him that radiated through my thin black dress.

I was sure my face was on fire. Ryan just did the classic move on me, and maybe if he did that a few months ago I wouldn't have batted an eye, but I had spent the last six weeks thinking about his body against mine.

Trying my best to act cool, I kept my grip how he showed me to hold the stick and hit the ball. And to my surprise, it worked. Two of the solid balls managed to find their way to pockets. I did a small clap in celebration before turning around to throw my arms around his shoulders. Plenty of people had tried to teach me how to play this game before (pool and darts were often the only entertainment at parties in our town), and I'd never actually sunk a shot on the first try.

We continued the game with us taking turns and Ryan wrapping his arms around me a few more times to 'show me' how I was doing things incorrectly. I let go of my embarrassment about my pink cheeks in favor of being happy about my improving performance. After I sunk the final shot, Ryan wrapped his arms around my stomach and lifted me in a quick spin. I could practically hear a crowd roaring in the background and a gold medal around my neck.

When he set me back down, I turned to find all of our friends staring at us with knowing smiles on their faces. The smile on my face dropped a little to sheepishly grab Charlotte and Georgia to go outside for some fresh air.

"So, you and Bacon, huh?" Charlotte said cockily as we sat on pool chairs in the backyard.

"Bacon?" Georgia asked. "What the hell does that mean?"

I couldn't help but smile at the throwback reference. We

called Ryan 'Bacon' way back in high school because one day he brought cold bacon in a plastic bag for his lunch. It was stupid, but it stuck. Charlotte was pretty reserved back then, so I was happy to have an inside joke between the two of us.

"She means Ryan, it was a stupid joke from school," I explained. "And for the millionth time we're just friends."

Two accusations in one night seemed like a pattern. Sure, we got a little comfortable during the pool game, but that was something we would have done even if we never had sex. It was just a game of pool for heaven's sake. *Right?*

Georgia laid back on the chair to look up at the stars. Rosewood was a small enough town that you could see the stars pretty well at night, even in a suburb like this. It was a chilly, but clear night, and I found myself looking up at them too. It was a good reminder of how small my problems were in comparison to how big the universe we lived in could be.

Ryan showed me the constellations once, years ago. I wondered if he still remembered them.

"Why do you ask?" I blurted out. "I mean– about me and Ryan?"

I wanted to know where this was all coming from. We weren't acting any different to normal, except for maybe some blushing on my end from all the physical contact. Now, I wished I had gone full out on my Elphaba costume and painted my face green, too.

Georgia and Charlotte stared at each other for a minute before Charlotte took the reins.

"You're acting like a couple, dude. No doubt about it," she said flatly.

Huh. That was a first. I couldn't help but wonder if it was the alcohol clouding her judgment. Georgia piped up to smooth things over, "You both seem happy."

When I stayed silent, she stood and helped me up, despite being very pregnant. "It's fine if you don't have everything figured out, we're just happy you're happy."

I smiled at her sweet words and followed them back inside. Another problem for another day. Ryan's eyes found me the second we walked back through the door, and I started to realize that maybe we were in a little over our heads.

As we walked outside to head home, I turned to him. "Do you think anyone knew? Were we acting differently?"

He scrunched his eyebrows together in confusion. "No, we were totally normal. Why do you ask?"

Chapter 8

Reese

End of the year exams were always the worst. Kids constantly coming in, asking to redo assignments from months ago, extra credit work to grade, and parents constantly calling and emailing. It was enough to make anyone sick to their stomach. And it was certainly getting to me this year.

I closed my laptop and looked at the clock to find that it was seven. Great, I would have to walk out to my car in the dark again. My bags in hand, I stood up to be met with another wave of nausea before hurrying out the door to head home and continue doing more work.

I slammed my apartment door closed and dropped my bags as gently as I could manage. Stomping through the house, I offered Ryan a quick hello on my way to the shower. I felt, and was sure I looked, like a drowned sewer rat. Today was really not my day.

The water took its sweet time heating up, so I sat on my toilet and focused on deep breaths while I waited. It was hard to focus on breathing when I was still shivering from the rain outside.

Ryan knocked on the bathroom door, and his muffled voice traveled through it. "Are you okay?"

"Peachy," I called back. Everyone has bad days, this one was just a little worse than usual.

My answer must have satisfied him because I heard his footsteps retreating back into the living room. We had done a great job over the last month and a half since The Incident. Other than Halloween, there was no questionably flirty physical contact. I made sure of that after thinking about Charlotte and Georgia's comments, but it just naturally didn't happen again. I was beginning to think there was something about being around our friends that made us slip into borderline more than friends behavior.

We were officially back to normal in our friendship. Sure, it was bound to be a little weird at times, but there was no passive aggressiveness or resentment. Ryan and I were still best friends, just with some complicated undertones.

He made sure not to overstep boundaries, we only went out to dinner together if our friends were involved. If we got invited to an event, he made sure not to be home before it so we always drove in separate cars. If something needed cleaning or replacing, he would help around the apartment, but made sure not to walk in my bedroom unless he had to go to the bathroom. We had the roommate act down to a science at this point.

My warm shower (not hot, our water heater never went past slightly warm) rejuvenated my soul to the point where I felt I could knock out some essays without pulling my hair out.

I joined Ryan in the living room where he was watching some international volleyball match and sat down next to him on my futon. *Our* futon? Ryan had bought it, but it was in my apartment. The semantics didn't really matter much.

"What are you working on tonight?" he asked. He sounded cautious, I assumed because my temper tantrum walking in the door raised some red flags.

"Just some essays," I mumbled. The first that I picked from the pile was one of my best students, and for that, I was grateful.

Ryan picked up the next in the pile, and I watched to see what he would do. He met my eyes and gestured with the paper. "Can I help?"

"They're essays, there isn't a right or wrong answer on these."

He grabbed a spare pen from the table. "You've been working nonstop, and I am capable of reading."

This was new. In our time since The Incident he hadn't asked to help with my work. It wasn't something he wouldn't do for a friend. If he asked any other time, I would've said absolutely not, but I needed a break today.

I went through a brief lesson on how to grade, what he should look for, and how to score them. He seemed confident after I told him to air on the side of leniency when it came to spelling or grammar.

We sat in mostly silence after he muted the volleyball match so he could focus, minus the odd question he had. We were about an hour in when he interrupted the silence to inform me of a common pattern.

"This is the third kid that started their essay with 'We live in a society,'" he griped.

I laughed quietly, not looking up from my paper. "They love that phrase, it fits almost any scenario. Plus, we *do* live in a society," I defended jokingly.

Finishing the paper I was on, I stood to go to the kitchen.

We were almost through with these essays, so I should have peace of mind knowing one of my biggest grading sessions of the semester was almost over. But my stomach still wouldn't settle.

"Do you want some tea?" I asked.

Ryan's face scrunched in disgust. "No, thanks."

Ginger tea was something my mother swore by, from the time I was a small child until high school. She claimed it could cure all, from a headache to a stomach ulcer, but somehow, she still always found herself sick. I drink it nowadays more out of habit than anything.

I brought the steaming mug back to our coffee table so the tea could steep while I started the next paper. My eyes started glazing over before I got through the first paragraph, so I let out a breath and decided to do more deep breathing while waiting for my tea to finish.

"I've never seen you drink that before," Ryan said.

I nodded with my head tilted back on the couch and eyes closed. "It's supposed to help with nausea and headaches."

"Are you sick?"

I sighed. "It's probably just stress or a stomach bug from one of my kids."

He sat quietly while I counted my breaths. I just wish this would all go away, it would soon enough anyway. Winter break was right around the corner. All I had to do was survive these next couple of weeks.

"You should rest, I can finish these."

I opened one eye to shoot him a look. "You don't need to do that, the tea will help."

With that, I sat up and took out the tea bag to sip it slowly. It warmed my throat and opened my sinuses, ginger tea tasted awful, but it always held a certain nostalgia. Especially in winter time. My mom always made sure to tell me that she drank it daily when she was pregnant with me. She said I made her so sick, even after the first trimester.

And I suspected she had been sick ever since then. Being pregnant-

Wait.

I sat up with perfect posture, as if someone cracked my spine like a glowstick to be straight as a ruler. Oh no.

"I need to go to the store." Panic threaded through my voice.

Ryan sat up slowly from where he was crouched in the corner of the futon. "Now?"

"Now." I shoved my shoes on with untied laces and grabbed my purse. "I'll be back in a bit."

My best friend crossed the living room and met me at the front door to press it shut. "Everything is closed, it's eleven, and we're in Rosewood."

"Oh." I stared back at him, a deer in headlights. I needed to go to the store. Now. Somewhere had to be open, I would drive to New York City if I had to. They say the city never sleeps, so surely a store had to be open there. It was only a measly six hours.

His eyes narrowed. "I think there's a 24-hour drug store in Charleston, will that work?"

Charleston! That was only thirty minutes, much quicker than my cross country road trip. I nodded my head and went to open the door again. His palm pressed against it stopped me.

"I'll drive," Ryan said. "Just let me grab my keys and put on some shoes."

"No, that's okay." I put on a smile to seem convincing, but

my voice gave away how nervous I felt. "I'll just go alone."

"I'm going with you Reese," he said firmly. He was looking at me like I was losing it. Maybe I was. "And I'm driving."

My hands were shaking again, and this time, it wasn't from the cold. It probably was best I let him drive, but he definitely wasn't allowed to go in the store with me. I needed to do this alone.

The ride there was silent after he asked what we were going for, and I wouldn't tell him. I felt his eyes shifting over to look at me every so often. I wasn't sure what he was looking for. All I could focus on was doing math in my head. It was hard to do calculations when it felt like sirens and bells were going off at the same time.

We pulled into the dimly lit parking lot, and it was empty except for a car parked at the back of the store. I turned to Ryan in a rush and told him, "You stay here."

I wasn't sure he would listen, but he did. I didn't give him much time to wait as I ran inside the store and sprinted through the aisles to find what I was looking for. The fluorescent lights nearly blinded me when I walked in and did nothing to help my nausea.

I grabbed the small box, and then doubled back to grab a few more in case one wasn't enough. The cashier made sure to stroll over to the register at the speed of a snail. As if the sky wasn't falling and I wasn't hyperventilating in an off-brand CVS at almost midnight on a Tuesday.

I left the receipt on the counter for him and shoved the bag into my purse so Ryan wouldn't see. He would obviously ask, but I wasn't capable of speaking until I knew for sure. I sat back down in the car and said nothing while I waited for him to drive us home.

"You're not going to tell me why we needed to come here on a second's notice?" He asked while staring at me.

"It doesn't matter." My red nail polish was peeling at the corners, so I took the liberty of scraping the rest of it off with my nails.

He grumbled something under his breath that I couldn't hear over the ringing in my ears and turned the car on to take us home.

When we got back, I quickly walked to my bedroom and shut the door. I poured out my purse on the bed and took stock of all the different brands of pregnancy tests. The electric one seemed like a safe bet, that way I wouldn't lose my mind over trying to see a pink line or not. It was just a fact, 'Pregnant' or 'Not Pregnant'.

I sat on the bed and rested my head in my hands. I couldn't actually be pregnant, we used a condom. This was all just a precaution, I was being paranoid. With my self-pep talk complete, I stood with my shoulders back and my head held high and marched into the bathroom with a test.

Sitting on the toilet with your pants around your ankles isn't the way you want your best friend and potential baby daddy to find out about your pregnancy scare. I heard Ryan knocking on my bedroom door before I realized I forgot to lock it. I finished peeing for the thirty seconds the test required before cleaning myself and locking the bathroom door when I heard him enter my bedroom.

I held my breath and pinched the bridge of my nose while I waited to hear what his reaction would be. Maybe if I concentrated hard enough, I could change forms and slide through the floor into the depths of the Earth, never to be seen or heard from again. Maybe-

"Reese, are you pregnant?" I could hear him clinging to his composure. He had the same tone that I would use to talk people off of ledges.

I rested my head back against the bathroom door. Three minutes felt like forever, and I forgot my phone in the other room, so I couldn't even time it.

"I don't know," I admitted. I almost repeated myself when he didn't respond, since I wasn't sure he could hear me through the door. My instinct was to take it all back, tell him this was all just a joke and everything would be okay. But he was Ryan, he always knew when I was lying.

"Will you please let me in?"

I took a step back and unlocked the door, he swung it open immediately and stood there in the gap. On the edge of no return. Now that I could see his face, I saw the fear in his eyes, and my instinct was to fix it.

"It's probably nothing, we used a condom. And I haven't slept with anyone else so," my voice trailed off. It didn't need to be said that I hadn't fucked anyone else. We shared the same shoebox of an apartment, he would have noticed if I brought someone home.

I had never seen him look so visibly uncomfortable. And he wasn't comfortable often. My reassurance did nothing but freak him out even further. My stomach felt even more uneasy, and I turned around to throw up in the toilet behind us.

He kneeled behind me to pull back my hair. How romantic. Through the sounds of my retching, I heard Ryan quietly telling me everything would be okay. *Of course it would, I'm not actually pregnant,* I thought. This would all be another embarrassing story Ryan would tease me about in a year or two, definitely not anytime too soon. It felt too real.

"I'll go grab you some water, okay?" he said. I wouldn't be surprised if he walked out of my apartment and never came back. I was such a mess, this was the most embarrassing moment of my life.

A cold glass of water was pressed into my hand soon after. He reached to push some sweaty strands of hair stuck to my forehead out of my face. I watched his eyes stray to the test still face up on the counter. Even with his height, he couldn't see the results over the counter edge from where we sat next to each other on the floor.

"Do you think it's done now?" he asked. "Or have you not done it yet?"

I took a big gulp of water. My sense of time was way off, he could have told me it'd been an hour or five minutes since we got back to my apartment, and I would have believed him.

"It's supposed to take three minutes. I'm not sure how long it's been."

He nodded. "Do you want me to look?"

No. Yes. I don't know. I just wanted to go to bed and wake up to find my stomach felt normal, and my world wasn't coming to a screeching halt.

"Sure," I mumbled.

"Whatever it says, we'll figure it out. Together," he said.

I nodded and watched him reach up to grab the test. He carefully avoided looking at it, and made eye contact with me to wait for another nod to confirm before seeing our fate.

His face told me all I needed to know. Half a second of reading his reaction and his eyes alone were enough. I let out a pitiful laugh and took another big gulp of water. It was like every ounce of panic flooded out of my body, and was replaced with acceptance. I needed to buckle in for the long haul.

81

"You're pregnant." I could tell he tried to steady his voice, but had failed miserably. He was shocked, probably horrified.

I just kept on sipping my water, at least throwing up made the nausea fade a little. Pregnant. I was going to have a baby. Or maybe not, I didn't have to. Something in me knew though, I was having this baby. I had always wanted to be a mother, but I, like the rest of the world, wanted the perfect scenario. A partner I loved. Perfect home. White picket fence.

"Reese," Ryan interrupted my thoughts. "You're pregnant." I looked up to find him staring at me with an emotion I didn't recognize. My own racing thoughts distracted me from trying to figure it out.

"I heard you."

"I know this is a lot, but I don't think it's a bad thing. In fact, I think it could be really great. There's no one else I'd rather have a child with." I just stared blankly at the floor. The words he said were going in one ear and out the other. "Are you okay? Can I get you something?"

"No, I'm pregnant, not sick."

He nodded and sat back down next to me, our backs against the wall and knees scrunched up because the bathroom was too small to fully spread them out. Like it was clockwork, my neighbors began banging their headboard against our adjoining wall. The faint sounds of moaning floated through the air soon after.

I started hysterically laughing. The kind of laugh that made my stomach hurt all over again, my abdominal muscles already sore from heaving. Ryan just looked at me with a sad smile.

My laughter died out when the banging echoed on. Who knows how long we sat there listening and feeling sorry for ourselves. Ryan stood up and offered me a hand.

"Come on, we can't sit here forever."

I took his hand, my butt hurt from sitting on the cold tile for so long. He led me into the bedroom, and I was ready to curl into a ball on the bed and try to sleep when he surprised me.

"Take off your shoes." I did as he said. "Now, come on."

He climbed on my bed and stood, the top of his head almost brushing the ceiling. I just stared up at him, confused. He reached for my arm to help me up, so we stood on the bed together. The squeaking of my neighbor's bed frame punctuating the silence.

I don't know what I expected Ryan to do, but jumping wasn't it.

He bounced on my bed, just hard enough for the bed to squeak loudly and slam into the wall. Just as loud, if not louder than my neighbor. I blinked at him in shock. Then he slapped the wall loudly, just to add to the act.

"Fuck!" Ryan yelled obnoxiously. I couldn't help but laugh, there was no way any of this was happening.

"Are you serious? This is so childish!" I whispered.

"Come on, they do this almost every night, they can fuck off."

I grabbed the headboard and joined him in shoving it against the wall with our weight before just bouncing on the bed for fun. We tried our best to hold back from laughing but failed miserably. The couple next door had done this for four years straight, tonight they would get payback.

I shrieked at the top of my lungs to mimic the woman's overly loud pornographic moans. At the sound of my shriek, Ryan and I both collapsed on the bed in laughter. We kept up the banging sounds until inevitably the neighbors took a hint and stopped.

I found myself staring at the ceiling again, just like right before The Incident that got me in this position. There was so much to think about that my brain felt overloaded, and not a single thought came through. Everything was quiet, and I wasn't sure how to feel, what to think, or what to do.

"I'm pregnant," I whispered.

Beside me, Ryan hummed. "We'll figure it out."

"What do you mean? What will we figure out? We aren't in a relationship, you're practically homeless, and we can't raise a baby in this apartment." I gestured at the general lack of space around us.

"I'm not homeless, honey. I can get us a house," he stated confidently. "Worst case, we can live with Jeeves in my apartment temporarily." He was so sure of himself, it was like he gave himself a moment to freak out in the bathroom, and now he was good. Solid. Unwavering.

"I'm not your honey, we're friends! Are we just going to live together forever?" He didn't respond. "Having a child together is more permanent than marriage. For the rest of your life, we'll have to make time for our kid together. Birthdays, holidays, graduations. Even if you hate me, for whatever reason, you'd have to suck it up for the sake of our child."

"Why would I hate you?" he sounded offended.

"I don't know! Things happen, people change. Point is, if I turned evil you would still have to deal with me because I'm your child's mother."

"I would never hate you, Reese."

"Whatever, you'd have to bring your trophy wife around to celebrate and they would have to see me. And you'd have to-"

"I don't plan on having anyone else to bring around," he said.

I huffed. Pushing hair out of my face, I turned back to him. "This is for life. For your entire life, we will be tied together. And not just together, to a *child*. Not just a baby, but a human being who will grow and need to be taught how to drive, and go to Kindergarten for the first time, and have their own thoughts and feelings and aspirations."

Ryan's hand fell to my cheek. He gently brushed his hand against my chin and tipped it up to hold eye contact with him. He didn't speak, just waited for a few breaths. I didn't realize I was practically out of air until I stopped talking.

"I understand," he affirmed quietly. "Do *you* want that?"

"What?"

"Do you want to have a child?" he asked. "With me."

I held his hand on my cheek and nodded. "You're my best friend, you're the only person I would trust to raise a child with. But it's obviously not ideal. Do *you* want to have a kid together?"

"Yeah, I think that would be nice."

My eyebrows shot up. "What?"

"I think it would be nice, you'd be a good mother." He paused, unsure if he wanted to continue. "I've always wanted to have a family."

Ryan Summers wanted a family? I had never heard him say that before. That seems like something that I, being his best friend, would have known. I always thought volleyball was his dream.

"What about your work? You're out of the country, like, a lot." My breathing picked up pace again. "That won't work."

He nodded and smoothed back my hair. I could tell he was thinking deeply, the crease between his eyebrows deepened when he was worrying or thinking hard. He reached behind me to grab his phone and look at the time.

"It will work." He got out of my bed and stood. "Do you want anything before bed? We don't need to figure everything out right now, and it's late."

I sat up. "What do you mean? You just want me to go to sleep?"

He hesitated by the bed. "Do you want to watch a movie?" His finger trailed along my bookshelf. "Or you can read?"

"We're having a baby. I can't just sit down and watch a rom com. There is *so much* to figure out."

"It's been a long day, we both just graded papers, and it's almost two in the morning. You should sleep."

I huffed and grabbed the book from my nightstand to glare at. There was no way I was actually going to sleep. Ryan sighed and walked out of my room. *How could he sleep like this?*

He walked back in a bit later with more water to find me still glaring at the same page. My eyelids were feeling heavy, and since he was always stealthy, he caught them falling.

"You're tired." He set the glass on my bedside table.

"I am not." I gripped the book tight.

After flicking the main light off and switching the lamp next to his side of the bed on, he sat back down next to me and reached for the book. "Let me."

"How will *you* reading help me?"

"Your eyes are closing, just relax." My eyebrows scrunched up together. What the hell was he-

Then he started reading. Out loud, he read the words to me starting from where I left off. His voice had always been soothing. The kind of voice you could listen to all day, no matter the topic he was going on about. I always thought it was such a shame he was never very talkative.

He read maybe four pages before my eyes closed for the final time, and I drifted off into the deepest sleep I ever had.

I woke up with a start. I was in my bed and alone. I must have had a nightmare because sweat soaked through my clothes, and my jaw hurt from clenching it so tightly. Then I noticed the light, oh shit. My alarm clock hadn't gone off, I always woke up before sunrise. From the looks of it, it was at least afternoon with how bright the sun was.

Tripping out of bed, I hurried to my bathroom to shower and did the quickest morning routine of my life. When I shoved the door to my bedroom open to grab my things and hightail it to school, Ryan stopped me in my tracks. He was sitting on the couch with the book he was reading to me last night.

That was when all the events of last night came rushing back to me. *Pregnant.* With my best friend's child. I was halfway through my spiral again when Ryan stopped me, yet again.

"I called your school and told them you're sick." His eyes flicked up to me over the top of the book.

"You what?"

"Called in sick. You could use a day off, regardless of our current circumstances," he reiterated.

I turned to start grabbing my things for school.

"What are you doing?"

"Going to school, there's a test today. I have to be there, I can't just miss school. I can't believe you called in sick for me."

"Reese, you should stay home. How are you feeling this morning?"

Not great, in fact, the question made me feel even more not-great. "I'm fine."

"Please don't go," he insisted. His tone of voice made me

stop. "You need to rest, you've been running yourself ragged. And I don't think I need to remind you, but you are pregnant. I can't stop you, but you really need to stay home."

"Okay." I would so regret this later. Never in my life had I called out sick from anything. But lately, I seemed to be having a lot of firsts.

Chapter 9

Ryan

My favorite person in the whole world. Pregnant. With my child. I expected that to be a much more clear cut happy moment in my life. And it was happy, but there were a lot more emotions that came with that.

I have no idea what the fuck I'm doing. Reese was curled up on the futon, head resting in my lap while I stroked her hair. It was more to calm myself than her as my mind reeled with everything that needed to be done. I opened my phone for the umpteenth time with a random question for Google about pregnancy.

We needed to schedule a doctor's appointment. I would bring that up to Reese when she woke up, but for now she needed rest. I was already concerned about her before, when she was only getting a few hours of sleep after work. The fact that she was pregnant sent that into overdrive.

How much sleep should a pregnant woman get a night? Google said a normal amount, but they might be sleepier during the day since they often don't get enough sleep at night. I took a look down at Reese again, yeah, that checks out.

There was so much to talk about, to decide. And here she laid, sleeping. Which was good, I wanted her to sleep, but I also wanted her to tell me we're doing this. All in, me and Reese for the rest of our lives. She seemed so caught up in the fact that I might want this, that she couldn't even decide if she wanted to raise a kid together for herself.

I only wanted to have a child if she did, I wouldn't tie her to me if she wasn't going to be happy. That would be my worst nightmare, having Reese and knowing I'm not good enough for her. Knowing I couldn't make her happy. Seeing her everyday and dulling her bubbliness.

Reese nuzzled her nose into the pillow on my lap and blinked awake. My dark thoughts must have disturbed her sleep, and I quietly cursed myself for that. I brushed the hair out of her face and admired her freckles. *She is so pretty. I would do anything for her.*

"Good morning," I mumbled.

She closed her eyes again and pulled the blanket higher so all of her was covered except her head. "It's definitely afternoon."

"Okay, you grump, apologies for the mistake," I said with a smile on my face. "Afternoon, to you."

She giggled into the blanket. "I guess afternoon does sound too formal."

"Mmhm," I agreed. "How are you feeling?"

I was caught off guard when she said she was nauseous last night. I had no idea she was feeling bad yesterday other than the fact that she was upset. I just thought that was because she got rained on. I needed to pay more attention, clearly I was missing a lot, if she came to the conclusion that she was pregnant and I had no idea.

"Fine," she said. "A little nauseous."

"Do you want some of that dirt tea again? It didn't seem to help much last time." She laughed again. I was doing much better today.

"No, I think I just need water and I'll be good."

I helped her sit up, so I could go grab it for her and returned to find her curled up in the corner of the futon, in my spot. I pushed the glass into her hand.

"We need to make you an appointment at the doctor's," I started. "Do you already have an OB GYN or do we need to find one?"

She cocked an eyebrow at me. "I have one. I can make the appointment now, I guess." I gave her some quiet while she messed around on her phone to eventually call someone.

"We should also talk about everything else," she said once she was done. "Like how we're going to coparent, custody, finances, all that jazz."

Custody? We were on very different pages. "Well, for one I want to be there for the kid like a real parent. No every other weekend bullshit."

"Okay, how will that work with volleyball?"

"Volleyball can wait."

"You told me you were asked to join the *Olympic* team. That's not an option."

"We would just be training for the year after next, I could commute, it's only a couple hour drive from here."

"Every day? You're going to drive two hours there and back every day to train?"

"It's not every day, it would just be some days," I answered.

"What about living arrangements then?"

"What about them?" I asked.

Reese pointedly did a full 180 to look around at the apartment we were sitting in. "We can't raise a baby here, and I can't afford much nicer on a teacher's salary."

"I already told you, I'll buy a house." I stole her glass to take a sip of water. "You just need to decide where, I assume you want to raise our kid in Rosewood?"

It was more of a rhetorical question, of course Reese would want to stay in Rosewood. Her family and friends all lived here. She grew up here, and had fond memories. Not to mention, she practically ran this town, people's lives would fall apart without her saving the day all the time.

"I think so, do you have somewhere else you think would be better? I also can't just let you buy a house, I have some savings that I could pitch in." Her lip pulled between her teeth told me she was just being polite.

"No, I think Rosewood is good, and I am definitely buying the house."

"I don't want this just to be a transactional thing, we're friends. I don't want to lose that, and I think our child would benefit from us staying friends."

"I can buy a house for us to live in, and remain friends with you, Reese."

"Isn't that a little sugar daddy-like though?" She panicked at the look on my face. "Not that that's a bad thing, it's just not my thing. It could complicate our friendship."

"I'd be buying the house for both of us and our child, Reese. So no, I wouldn't be your sugar daddy."

"But you are my baby daddy," she argued.

"Let's table that for now." I keep going in circles like this. "What else are you worried about?"

We continued on like that for hours, at one point I got out a pen and piece of scratch paper to write down things for us to research and talk about again later. Pros and cons, things we needed to learn, people we needed to tell. The paper filled up quickly, and I was starting to see why Reese had trouble falling asleep last night.

"So we need to do all of this before the baby is here," I recapped. My eyes scanned through the papers filled with my chicken scratch.

Reese's eyes followed mine and she nodded, looking worried. I wrapped my arm around her shoulders to reassure her. Then I pressed my lips to her head softly and considered our next move.

She shuffled away from me. "I think we should also be clear about boundaries, we're two very good friends figuring out how to raise a child together. Adding a new relationship on top of that probably isn't the best idea."

"Right." I could take a hint. No more forehead kisses. "We will stay friends, but I want to be clear that this isn't all going to be on you. I'm an equal partner in raising our child."

"Of course," she said confidently. "We make a good team. And I can't imagine doing all of this alone."

Standing up, I reached my hand out to her to help her up. "We'll take care of it. At least we know all we need to do now."

I ushered her to the entryway and handed her the black converse she liked to wear most. My old beat up sneakers were pulled on and tied while she stared down at me.

"What are we doing? I'm not really in the mood to go for a CPR course or look for houses right now."

"We're going for a walk." I waited for her to sit and slip the shoes before tying them up. "I think we've sat on the couch enough for today. Fresh air will do us some good."

We were out by the lake, sitting in the grass and watching

ducks swim by. I made the mistake of not reminding Reese to bring a jacket, so I gave her my sweatshirt to keep her warm. That was definitely something I would do for a friend.

"Did you do well on that flour baby project in high school?" Reese asked with a smile.

I snorted. "I try to forget mine, I was paired with Sandra Collins and she busted our baby open in less than a day."

Her laugh danced in the breeze. "I didn't know that, but it sounds about right. Where were you when the baby broke?"

"At practice," I defended. "I only left her alone with it for an hour."

"Well you probably shouldn't have referred to your baby as an 'it'. Did you at least name them?"

"Roulf." She gave me a funny look. "It's flour backwards."

"Ah, poor Roulf. My baby survived the full week, I was paired with Sam B, though, so it wasn't exactly an easy feat."

I remembered, I spent that full week annoyed that Sam found his way into every hangout our friend group had. Even going so far as to join Reese in watching our volleyball practice. And the idiot never failed to mention his 'wife and kid'. I wanted to punch the kid in the face.

"Well at least one of us has shown some promise in being a good parent."

Reese whipped her head to look at me. "You'll be a great dad."

"What makes you think that? I didn't exactly have the best example." Or any example. "I guess I can only improve from what I had."

"You're willing to try," Reese insisted. "You've already done more in the last twelve hours than most dads do."

I scoffed. It was sweet, but I doubted that.

"I mean it, trying is most of what matters in parenting. At school, the kids that have reliable parents that check in regularly and show up to parent teacher nights always do the best."

She picked at a weed before throwing it toward the lake. "Besides, I think a lot of parenting is learned through trial and error. No one is just born a good parent, and we have time to study all we need."

Chapter 10

Reese

The locker room of the local gym in Rosewood was surprisingly clean. I signed up for this class a month ago when one of my students' grandmother recommended it. Water aerobics seemed like fun, I had no idea what it really was, but I knew how to swim.

Georgia sat on the bench next to me, belly ready to pop. She managed to work out throughout her entire pregnancy, and I was truly amazed. I couldn't keep a regular exercise routine ever, but being pregnant seemed like a good enough reason to start.

"So, have you ever done this before?" she asked.

"No, but it should be fun." I tied up my hair so it wouldn't get wet. "And it's low impact, so it should be perfect for being nine months pregnant."

"Eight, but thanks for the reminder," she griped. "Has anything new been going on with you lately?"

Sometimes women asked questions that they already knew the answer to. This absolutely one of those times. Georgia's mouth turned up as she waited for my response.

"Yeah, actually," I said carefully. How did people tell their friends they were pregnant? Should I have planned this out? Bought a present? I should make an excuse and redo this later. When Ryan and I discussed telling people, we mainly talked about our families.

"I'm pregnant," I whispered. We were the only two people in the locker room without hearing aids, but better to be safe.

Georgia's jaw dropped, and I did my best to give her a sufficient amount of time to process without word vomiting at her. I hadn't told anyone else other than Ryan yet, and I was dying to talk to anyone about it that would listen.

"Oh. My. God." Her eyes were as wide as saucers. "And it's- and you-"

"Ryan's. Yeah." I squeezed my hands together and waited for her to freak out more.

"Oh," she squeaked. She couldn't even muster up a 'My' or 'God' anymore. Georgia was fully and completely speechless.

She let out a breath and her smile formed before throwing her arms around my shoulders. "Oh my God!"

"Yeah, got that." I laughed.

"You're pregnant," she repeated breathlessly. "I'm pregnant. We're both having babies! This is amazing, I'm so happy for you."

She saw the hesitance on my face. "We are happy right? Or are we still figuring things out. Oh my God, I'm so sorry."

I put my hand on her shoulder to stop her. "We're happy. Still just getting used to it is all, I haven't told anyone else. Other than Ryan of course."

"Oh my God!"

We hugged again briefly when the herd of women started marching past us into the pool area. Based on how they were

97

dressed, Georgia and I were seriously underprepared. They had matching waterproof caps and visors to go with their bathing suits.

"I want every detail the second we get out of this pool," Georgia said.

We shared another look and squeeze of hands before laughing together and headed into the pool for our first water aerobics lesson. Turns out, the local water aerobics class didn't get new classmates often. The second we joined the mature women in the pool, we were suddenly the stars of the show. I tried my best to jump in for Georgia since she can be a little shy. When one of the less self aware ladies tried to reach out to feel her stomach, I did my best swan dive to block it and pointed to the instructor that was desperately trying to get everyone's attention.

Georgia and I spent most of our time watching what the other ladies did and tried to mimic it. For the most part, it just looked like various forms of flailing limbs under the water. But to their credit, it was a great core workout.

Midway through class, I felt someone's eyes on me. I did a quick swivel to find all of the ladies focused on their own exercising. Brushing it off, I returned back to my awkward kicks while using the pool noodle to support my upper half.

Then I saw Ryan's tall frame out of the corner of my eye. Whoever decided to put wall to wall windows in the pool area, so the entrance of the gym could see the entire pool when coming and going, had a sadistic streak. It wasn't until I saw Ryan and Nick staring at us from the hallway that I realized exactly how dorky this activity was.

Ryan gave a small wave, and I could tell from the faint smile that flirted with his lips he would absolutely be bringing this up later. I cringed and gave a small wave back before tapping Georgia so she could wave also. I expected them to leave after acknowledging the situation, but Ryan crossed his arms and leaned back against the hallway to keep watching for longer.

It took me mouthing "Get out!" and pointing toward the exit of the gym for him to take a hint. His smirk made me blush a little, and he blew a pretend kiss to seal the deal. Nick trailed behind him, and I could already predict the sarcastic quip that came out of our friend's mouth.

After class, ladies swarmed around us in the locker room. My student's granny that recommended the class gave me another full explanation of how water aerobics helped her recover after her double knee replacement. We were in there for about an hour before another night swimming class started trailing in, which was very clearly a different (younger) demographic.

With promises to come back, we exited the door and hurried toward my car to debrief. Once in the car, Georgia turned her body to face me as much as physically possible.

"Sooooo, you and Ryan?" her smile was megawatt.

"Me and Ryan. Having a baby." I turned the car key, and we were on our way to Georgia's house. "No big deal."

She scoffed. "This is, like, decades in the making, so yeah no big deal." Her hand reached over to hold my elbow and squeeze. "Tell me everything!"

We sat in my parked car for at least an hour in the driveway of Georgia and Ashton's house. There was a lot to talk about, and there was no better place to lay out everything I had held in for months than my car. It was the perfect confessional.

"Oh hold on, Ash is texting me asking where I am," Georgia said.

I took time to pause and check my own phone. One missed call from Ryan. I texted him that I would be home soon. That was the friendly thing to do.

"Okay, so, you're friends, but parenting together? Not dating."

"Right, no romantic relationship. I think we're just meant to be friends."

"Why? I think you would both be great together. It's clear you have chemistry." She gave me a sly smile. "In more ways than one." "

I sighed. "I wouldn't want to force a relationship just because I'm pregnant, it's not like this is 1980."

"That's really not that long ago," Georgia pondered. "And would the relationship just be for the baby? No offense, but Ashton says you two have been a 'will they, won't they' for a long time."

"It's official, *they* won't," I finalized. "There is so much other stuff we have to figure out. And on top of all of that, I don't want to risk losing my friendship with him. If we dated and it didn't work out, I wouldn't be able to stay friends with him. That's too much to handle."

Georgia rested her hand on top of mine that sat on the gear shift. "It must be scary. No matter what, you know, Ash and I are here for you."

"Thanks, George." I gave her hand a quick squeeze. "Worst comes to worst, I just end up being a single parent. Which wouldn't be the end of the world."

Dread filled my chest with enough force to break bones. It wouldn't be the end of *the* world, but it would definitely be the end of *my* world. I wanted to be a good mom, but I also wanted to still be my own person. That would be considerably

100

harder if I had to do everything on my own.

Georgia poured water over the flames. "Ryan will be there for you. He can be kind of self-centered sometimes, but never when it comes to you."

I nodded. "Hopefully, it's just hard to picture what that would look like. We both grew up with single mothers, so I think we're kind of lost on the whole coparenting thing."

"Well if you ever need practice you're welcome to babysit Ruth anytime. Especially after this baby arrives." She rubbed her stomach and gazed down at it lovingly.

"I might take you up on that," I said. "We should get you inside before Ashton starts peeking at us through the blinds."

Georgia laughed and looked over at the light flooding through the window on the porch. "I'm pretty sure he already has."

I got out of the car and carried her gym bag for her inside before saying goodbye to everyone and promising to take Ruth on a 'friend date' sometime soon. That was something we had done since before she could talk. There was a time that I was the only woman around in her life, and as Ashton's friend I made sure to be there for her.

Sighing, I sat in my car in silence for a few minutes before heading home. That went well, it was a good sign for when I had to tell my mother. Although that would have to wait, I couldn't tell her without a confirmed doctor's approval that everything was okay and healthy. Even then, she would likely make it about her and tell horror stories of her time being pregnant with me.

* * *

"I had no idea the mother of my child was into synchronized swimming," Ryan greeted as I walked through the door.

"It's water aerobics, very different," I snarked.

"My apologies, ma'am." He grabbed my bags from me to put in my bedroom. "Whatever it is, I'm a big fan. Is there an Olympic event for that? We should sign you up."

"We could be a power couple," I played along. "Two Olympic medalists raising a kid together."

I sat down and propped up my feet on the coffee table. "I told Georgia about the baby."

"Yeah?" he said mindlessly.

"Is that okay? I know we talked about waiting to tell our parents, but I wasn't sure what the policy was about friends."

"Of course it is, I trust your judgment."

"Have you told anyone?"

"No, not yet."

"So you went to the gym with Nick, did a whole," I paused to think about whatever it is they did. "Whatever. And never once mentioned the life changing event that happened this week?"

"He didn't ask." He walked back in the living room after he was done grabbing a water bottle for me. "And we were playing basketball, for the record. Not much time for talking."

"I will never understand men."

* * *

Last minute prepping and teaching for final exams was always the worst. I had been on my feet all day long, and even though I wasn't very pregnant, my feet were definitely swollen. They weren't kidding about that symptom.

I sat down during my last period and did my best to still be as interactive to keep everyone's attention. Slipping off my boots, I leaned back during a quiet moment for them to collaborate and go over each other's answers for their practice test. The nausea did nothing to help my situation either.

I remembered I had an emergency pack of saltine crackers in my desk drawer and pulled them out to hopefully settle my stomach. I hated eating in the classroom, kids always made a big deal of it and asked me to share. Which was fair, I had a rule for that reason to only eat if I brought enough to share with the kids. In this case though, I suspected they would prefer I eat some crackers than run to the bathroom to puke.

After hours, I was doing some last minute planning for the last week of school before break. One more week. Five days. I could make it through this.

My phone rang and interrupted my last tweaks to the schedule. Ryan's name popped up and I answered it.

"Hey, are you still at school?"

"Yeah, just doing a few last things, and then I can head home."

"Are you feeling better than you did this morning? I texted you during lunch, but you never answered."

"Oh, sorry, it's been a crazy day." I rubbed my stomach and started to slip my boots back on with a groan. "I'm okay, could be better."

"Stay there, I'll come and pick you up."

"You don't have to-" Ryan hung up the phone on me.

I was wrapped up in writing a college letter of recommendation for one of my previous students when he showed up at my classroom. Smiling at him, I set my laptop to the side and stood up to greet him. I really needed a hug after such a long day.

He was stiff, but allowed me to hug him. He hesitated before raising his arms to wrap around me and hold me close. I let out the breath I was holding in and backed up to lean against my desk.

"Feet hurt?" he asked.

"Oh," I looked down at my mismatched-sock covered feet on the carpet and felt my cheeks heat up. "Yeah, I forgot I took my shoes off."

"Just sit, let's get all of this packed up." I happily listened to his order, I would wait till the very last minute to shove my feet back into those damn boots.

When I had everything sorted and put away just how I liked, he swung my backpack over one shoulder and my giant tote over the other. I reached for my boots again, but Ryan stopped me.

"Just wait here, I'll be right back."

I waited, a little confused. I assumed he was grabbing something quickly from the hall, but minutes passed with no return from him. I spun around in my desk chair a few times before realizing that was a silly thing to do when nauseous.

Ryan appeared back in the doorway empty handed.

"Alright, hop on." He spun around and crouched down in front of me. "Oh, and hand me those."

His hand reached out for my boots, and I gave them over to him. "You want to give me a piggyback ride?"

"Yeah, come on."

"I'm too heavy, we're grown adults, you can't just give me a piggyback ride."

His eyebrows raised. "You really think I can't carry you?"

"Well I'm sure you *can,* I'm not sure you *should.*"

He turned around, sick of my arguing and decided to scoop

me up out of my chair, carrying me bridal style.

"Ryan!"

"You've been here for over twelve hours, we're going home." He ignored my blatant protest of him carrying me.

I sighed, giving in. "Can we get ice cream?"

"Absolutely, we'll get some on the way home."

* * *

My ice cream started melting down the sides of the cone and getting my fingers all sticky. I did my best to lick it up to avoid making even more of a mess when I caught Ryan watching me with a quirked eyebrow. My cheeks heated, and I reached for a napkin sitting on the dash.

"You need to take it easy when it comes to work. These people walk all over you, and if you're overwhelmed, you need to be able to say no."

I rolled my eyes subtly while continuing to eat my ice cream. "I don't mind helping other people when they need it."

"But you are going through a lot right now, we have a lot of big, stressful changes coming up, so you need to be able to leave time for yourself."

"There's plenty of time in the day to do all the things I need to do." A white lie. I glanced over at Ryan to see him glaring at me. "Okay, I'll work on it."

"I'm serious. It's not healthy to be stuck in that building for twelve hours a day." He grabbed another napkin and wiped off my chin. "That goes for the baby too, if you don't care enough about yourself, think about them."

"I hear you. I'll stop leaving so late every day. And I can talk to my principal about the extra work she's been giving me."

"Good," he affirmed. "Then you'll have more time for fun stuff, like your synchronized swimming." He snorted at the thought. "Next, we should take you to bingo night, I hear it's all the rage these days."

"I'm only twenty eight, and it's *water aerobics*."

Chapter 11

Ryan

Never in my life had I felt so nervous. Suddenly, I realized the past few weeks were child's play compared to what was coming. This was real, and Reese needed me to be reliable. I had never been called reliable for anything other than scoring points in a volleyball match.

Ashton did this all on his own. Not the pregnancy part, the fathering part, I should have asked him for advice. Reese was practically born knowing everything, and while Google helped a good amount, at this point I was realizing I didn't even know what questions I should ask.

I leaned against the off-white countertop of Reese's kitchen and waited for coffee to finish brewing. My urge to move out of this place was strong. Buying a house for her was one of the few things we still hadn't come to a compromise on. She wanted to at least pitch in a quarter of the down payment which just wasn't enough for any of the homes we liked. She would cave eventually and see things my way. At least, I hoped she would.

Reese strolled into the kitchen, looking just as nervous as I felt. She was dressed in a pretty green dress, and her hair was put up with one of those clips with teeth. I was dumbstruck by her, she was carrying my baby. Mine. I resisted the urge to hold her by the hips and bring her close by filling my hands with two mugs.

"Oh, that's nice but I can't drink coffee," Reese said.

I turned to face her. "It's decaf, the internet says small amounts of decaf are okay. But if you want to wait until we ask the doctor, that's okay too."

"Should've known you asked Google," she joked. "I didn't realize I had any decaf."

"You didn't, I bought it the other day when I picked up your juice." She took the mug hesitantly. "It's got whipped cream on top and cinnamon in it."

That perked her up. "One day, you'll have to teach me your weird iced coffee recipe," I reminded. "For now, I figured this was the safest option."

* * *

We sat in the waiting room, Reese's knee bouncing uncontrollably. I rested my hand on it to stop her panicking. She shot me a tense smile. Apart from us, the room was completely empty. It would be nice to have other people here, so I could see what we should be doing. I couldn't help but wonder if it was normal to be this nervous.

"Are you sure that was decaf?" Reese did her best to break the deafening silence.

I rubbed my thumb over her kneecap, more to soothe myself than her. "It was. I'm about ready to run a marathon right now, though." I shuffled in my seat. "Why the hell do they have to keep it so cold in here? Are you cold?"

She nodded. "It's even colder than they keep it at school."

I watched Reese pull her sleeves down over her hands. Instead of letting her freeze, I grabbed both of her palms and rubbed them before blowing air into our cupped hands. Women were always cold, why the hell would a gynecologist keep the thermostat at sub arctic temperatures.

"Why are we having to wait so long?" I grumbled.

"Don't be so grumpy, they probably overbooked." She gently pulled her hands back to cross her arms over her chest. "I should have brought a snack or something, I'm starving."

I stood up and stalked out of the room, happy for the excuse to get out of that cold plastic chair. When I returned, Reese's posture straightened at the sight of some chips I got from the vending machine. She took them happily and popped open the bag with haste.

"Do you want any?" she asked.

"No, thanks." Even though I hadn't eaten yet today, my stomach was turning itself into knots enough from stress to make me forget the hunger pangs.

A tall woman in navy blue scrubs peeked her head into the room to call, "Reese!"

Reese, with a chip in her mouth, waved before standing up and grabbing her bag. I stood slowly, unsure of what I was supposed to do in this situation. Do men go back there for these appointments? I was so in over my head.

Reese and the nurse were catching up (of course Reese knew everyone here personally) when I interrupted, "Do I go with her? Or do I stay here?"

"You can stay here if you don't want to," Reese whispered. "I understand if it's overwhelming."

109

"I'm asking if I can go with you, I want to be there."

The nurse giggled at my awkwardness and ushered us both forward into the hallway. "You're both welcome, come on back."

She guided us to our own room and left us alone once again, not without a promise to see Reese at the next book club.

"Is there anyone in this town you aren't friends with?" I mumbled. The posters on the wall were filled with warnings of preventative tests.

Reese didn't answer, so I turned to look at her. I found her smiling at me, knowingly. "You're nervous."

"Of course I am, I have no idea what I'm doing."

I hated being bad at things, loathed it even. In fact, I often went out of my way to avoid things that I wasn't familiar with, so I didn't risk being bad at them. That was why being an athlete was the center of my universe, it was what I was good at.

"Neither do I, we'll figure it out together." Reese reached for my hand and looked into my eyes with all the faith in the world. She trusted me to do this. I just needed to live up to her expectations.

The doctor walked in, and I felt like I was in a fever dream. I did my best to pay attention but in the end didn't retain any information whatsoever. I was so focused on the little screen showing blurry black and white shapes that it was hard to hear. My hand found Reese's as we waited impatiently.

"There's your baby," the woman said.

Reese squeezed my hand tightly, and I spared a glance at her to see tears welling up in the corners of her eyes. I didn't realize I was crying too until she reached up with her free hand to wipe my cheek. That was our kid. Fuzzy pixels on a screen.

"Do we get to keep a picture?" I asked. I regretted making fun of Ashton before. This little blob deserved to be plastered across town. I wanted to carry it with me to show everyone I came across.

"Of course, I'll take a couple for you."

"They're so beautiful. I can't believe that's our baby." Just hearing Reese acknowledge the baby was ours made my heart beat impossibly faster. Our own little family. It was better than anything I'd imagined in my wildest dreams.

Chapter 12

Reese

When I volunteered to puppysit for Charlotte, I was more so thinking about how cute Luma was than how much effort and energy a puppy requires. Also, I didn't know I would be pregnant. And emotional.

Luma was a fluffy blonde ball of pure joy. Her counterpart, Link, was content to laze around all day and walk at my pace, which was pretty relaxed. I sat on the bench near the lake and couldn't help but compare those two to Ryan and me. Link laid down in the grass while Luma was bouncing around from one end of the leash to the other, getting herself tangled around the legs of the bench I was sitting on.

The cats watched us from a distance, clearly skeptical of the chaos that was Luma. Even the ducks were up on the bank, watching near the cats while resting on the grass. This was the one, and only, time I had ever seen the two in a joint task force.

Tears welled up in the corners of my eyes as I watched Luma get her leash wrapped around her legs yet again. I was so in over my head. The puppy kept pulling away as I reached to untangle her. *She's just a puppy, she doesn't know better.* Wait. If I'm getting this worked over a puppy, *how would I handle a literal child?*

I sniffled and rubbed my nose with the sleeve of my over-sized sweater. The kids at school still didn't know I was pregnant yet, and my bump was finally becoming visible. It was both a relief and another hurdle for me to jump over to hide.

Ryan's car pulled up in the parking lot to our apartment, it was only a few yards from the lake-front bench I was sitting on. I quickly turned to cover my face and swipe off the tears building in my lashline. He had been so patient with me these last few weeks. I knew taking care of others didn't come very easily to him, but it was clear he was trying, and for that, I was grateful.

As he walked toward us, Luma jumped to the end of the leash to greet him. The force of her pulling nearly yanked me off the bench, but I gritted my teeth and held on. Link, who could definitely pull me off of the bench if he tried, lazily stood and wagged his tail quietly waiting for his favorite person. The dogs both loved Ryan, even if he never tried with them. All they ever wanted from me was treats.

"I brought you some candy," Ryan said.

I did my best to pull off a convincing smile and took his offering. "Thanks," I greeted.

"Here," Ryan gently took the end of the leashes from me and sat down. His thigh brushed against mine, and I couldn't help but lean my head on his shoulder. His long arm wrapped around my shoulders and rested against my elbow.

"Rough day?" he asked.

I nodded. This entire week felt like a game. I kept running

113

to stay on track, but the faster I ran the faster everything kept flying at me while the finish line got further and further away. Figuring out Thanksgiving, making sure my students had all they needed before the holiday break, and researching how to be a parent, were all a balancing act.

"We should do something fun," he said, looking to me for a reaction. "We still have time to catch the sunset at the beach if we leave now."

"Luma will just get sand everywhere," I mumbled. She sat calmly at our feet now, placated by Ryan's hand petting her head.

"We can leave the dogs behind. I think we've puppy proofed your apartment enough to leave them alone for a bit."

"I can't just leave them. What if they get hurt, or escape or something."

Ryan leaned toward me and jerkily stopped himself before standing up. Every interaction we had recently felt so intimate, I wasn't sure if it was pregnancy hormones or me that was reading into things. We were just friends having a baby together. No big deal.

"I'll be right back, you keep watch of the ducks," he ordered.

He returned, no puppies in sight, and led me to his car. I felt empty, no energy left to care about how selfish it is to leave a puppy alone in an apartment. Or to care about poor Link who was left alone with his annoying younger sibling. Definitely no energy to worry over if they would chew up our cables, or get to a lithium battery somehow and create an explosion. Then that explosion would turn into a fire that could burn down the whole building. All the other families that would lose their homes or get hurt because I was selfish enough to leave a puppy unsupervised.

"I should go get them, they would love the extra exercise," I concluded.

"They've had enough exercise, I took them on a hike this morning and they came with me to play basketball earlier." Ryan gave me a side eye. "You need time without dogs or kids to worry about."

"What about when we have our kid," I demanded. "Are we just going to leave a newborn home alone to fend for herself?"

"You think we're having a girl?" he asked. His carefree tone sounded ridiculous directly in contrast to mine.

"Answer the question," I said.

"Of course not, dogs are a little different from a baby, Reese."

"Exactly!" I cried. "They're supposed to be *easier*, I can't even manage two dogs for a week, how on Earth will I take care of a child?"

His hand found mine and pulled it over the center console. "You're doing a lot more than taking care of two dogs right now, you have a million responsibilities. Anyone would be stressed out."

"I'll have all of those same responsibilities when we have a child," I pointed out.

We pulled to the white line at a red light and he looked over at me. "You don't have to."

"Of course I-"

"No," he interrupted. "You don't. You are the kindest person I have ever met, and people take advantage of that. The principal doesn't need you, a teacher, to do her work for her at school. The water aerobics grannies don't need you to create posters for their walkathon, they can figure it out themselves. And you didn't have to watch these dogs for Charlotte, she could have asked someone else."

115

I didn't realize I told him all of that. At least he listened to me, but I really *did* need to do all of those things. These were people that relied on me and I couldn't just refuse to help someone when they needed a hand. I wasn't wired that way.

"I disagree." My arms crossed over my chest.

He let out a long sigh. "How is anyone helping you?"

"What do you mean?"

"You're pregnant," Ryan looked at me expectantly. When I had nothing to add he continued, "This is one of the most stressful times in your life. A big moment, you have no idea what you're doing. No experience. How are any of those people helping you out in your time of need?"

"I don't need help," I defended. "I got myself in this situation."

"So did everyone else," he argued. "Charlotte and Nick didn't have to buy a puppy right before they went on their pre-honeymoon. Who even takes a vacation before getting married? That was their poor planning. And Nick has a perfectly good brother with a house and a backyard with plenty of space for them. You shouldn't have to house two dogs in your tiny apartment. It's a shitty thing to ask."

"She's one of my best friends."

"Then you should feel comfortable telling her no when something doesn't work for you."

I scoffed and pressed my forehead against the cool window. Fog formed from my breath on the glass. "We're just different, you'll never understand my reasoning for things."

"Maybe so, but you can't go on like this. You're running yourself into the ground, Reese."

"I'm just a little tired. Can we drop it for now please?" He let out a frustrated groan, but listened to my request and turned up his music.

116

* * *

The next morning, I felt much more at peace. Turns out fresh air and a beautiful sunset could do a lot of good for my mind. We were starting to get a consistent morning routine with the dogs. Ryan took them for a walk while I slept in since it was a Saturday, and I woke up refreshed and carefree. I was humming to my early 2000's playlist when I heard a loud crash.

"Luma," Ryan's loud groan made my good mood come to a rapid halt.

I stood in the doorway of the kitchen to find an entire milk carton on the floor along with a half opened egg carton with broken eggs next to it. Ryan turned to me, his face annoyed but handsome as ever.

"Just go in the living room. I'll take care of it."

Luma then dove for the eggs. Ryan caught her in time, but not before Link stalked through the milk to start licking up raw egg from the ground. I leaned down to hold him back. In the chaos, Luma got away and carried her milk soaked paw prints throughout the carpet floors of the rest of the apartment.

"I'll take care of it," Ryan reassured before brushing past me to catch the culprit.

Half an hour and several tears caused by spilled milk later, Ryan collapsed on the couch beside me. He let out a dry laugh and covered his face with his palm. The veins of his forearms caught my attention while I tried to figure out what to say.

"We should go house hunting today."

I had no argument for that, there was not enough room for the two of us in here. And if the dogs were any sign, we needed more space for a baby too. The last few days, all four of us were constantly on top of each other, which definitely wasn't helping my stress levels.

Chapter 13

Ryan

Reese seemed more interested in making friends with our realtor than actually looking at any houses. She walked through each room, a constant state of motion with her head on a swivel. Nothing was ever appealing enough to catch her gaze and make her stop, and I was beginning to wonder if that was because of the price tag attached.

"What do you think of this one? The backyard is nice," I said while trailing behind her.

She hummed noncommittally. "Yeah, it's a nice house. The flooring is absolutely stunning, and I like the neighborhood. Our kid could walk to school when they go to high school, and it's a short commute for me."

"But it's not our house," I concluded.

Reese shrugged and continued her meandering around every pathway possible in the home. Shannon, our realtor, got her caught up in another chat about windows and sunlight where they spoke passionately. Though I could tell from her face, this was not the house for Reese.

We got back in my car to head home after viewing almost a

dozen homes in the area. That was practically all the houses on sale in Rosewood, turns out, not many people like to move house right around the holidays.

"That house checked all our boxes, so what didn't you like about it?" I needed concrete answers to figure out what we were going to do. We couldn't spend our first Christmas together in that tiny ass apartment.

Reese squirmed in the passenger seat. "It just didn't feel right."

"Is this about money? Because again, it's not something you need to worry about Reese, I told you I'd take care of it."

"I don't want you to though," she said. I tried making eye contact, but her gaze was placed firmly on the window.

"Why not?"

"I don't need you to take care of me, if we're buying a house together it should be a joint effort."

"You're carrying our child, that isn't a joint effort. It's just you growing and creating life, so why can't I take care of the house on my own?"

"It's different," she huffed.

I pulled over into the nearest parking lot and waited for her to look at me. When she did, I grabbed her hand, so she could tell how sincere I was being. It was something I saw her do often with stubborn people who resisted her magical charms and wouldn't let her fix all of their problems.

"I can take care of you," I insisted. She opened her mouth to interrupt but I continued, "You take care of everyone else, let me do this for you. For us, even. And our baby."

She was silent. "Do you not trust me?" I asked.

"Of course I do."

"Then let me do this one thing," I urged. "Please."

She gave me a quick nod after deeply contemplating her options. I suspected there weren't many times in her life that Reese let anyone fully take over the responsibility to do something. When we were paired together in high school she always commanded projects and made sure to do more than her fair share. In adulthood, she always planned every birthday party, reminded others to congratulate friends for their achievements, and checked-in when she hadn't heard from someone in a while.

I tapped her chin for her to look at me again. My eyebrow quirked to encourage her to say it out loud, let me in and let me help. I wanted equal partnership in this operation, not to be some charity case boyfriend she took care of like she did everyone else.

"Okay, you can take care of it. But if it's too much I can-"

"I've got it, I promise," I finalized. Clicking my seatbelt, I got us back on the road to head home. A light bulb went off in my head, and I realized just what to do to get Reese the perfect home.

* * *

"And you would be willing to sign next week or so?" I asked.

The muffled voice over the phone agreed. My genius plan was a long shot, but it seemed to be working so far. We exchanged more information, so I could hand it off to my realtor before I got a notification that Reese was calling.

"Hey Jim, my-" What was I supposed to refer to Reese as? Baby mama? "My friend," I nearly choked trying to get the word out. "Is calling, I should answer to make sure everything is alright."

We hung up promptly after saying goodbye, so I could answer her. She didn't call me often, so my heart raced at the prospect of something being wrong. It was about time for her to come home anyway, maybe she was just asking if she should pick up something for dinner.

"Hey," she started. Her voice already sounded shaky, and my heart raced faster.

"Hey, is everything okay?"

"Yeah, are you busy or can you talk for a minute?" she asked.

"I've got all day," I soothed. "What's wrong?"

"It's just stupid work." I heard a sniffle through the phone. "My boss doesn't like that I've been leaving right after school this past week."

"Isn't that when you're supposed to be off? What does she need you to stay for?"

"Nothing, it's just she comes to ask for my help sometimes after school hours, and I haven't been here because we agreed I would take it easy."

She took a breath before explaining further, "I know I promised to come home after ten hours at work, but I don't think I can today."

My keys were already in my pocket as I started toward the parking lot, so I could get to her. There was no way I was letting some principal bully my pregnant, *baby mama*, into working extra hours. Someone needed a reality check.

"I'll come help you."

"It's not something you can help with," she assured. "It's research and a powerpoint presentation for the school board. It'll just take me a few hours, and I don't want you to worry."

The stress in her voice absolutely made me worry. "You're upset, and this isn't your job. Just stay there and we'll figure this out together, okay?"

She sniffled again. "Okay."

I stood in the doorway to Reese's classroom to find a very distraught pregnant woman with her feet propped up on a file cabinet. She cheered up at the sight of me and gave me a smile. My fury was temporarily soothed by the sweet smile on her face, but was reignited by the reminder that someone had caused those tear tracks down the sides of her cheeks.

"Is this project in any way part of your job description?" I asked.

"No, but she said if I still want the vice principal position-"

"Do you want that job?"

"It's a step up."

"But do you want it? You love teaching and working with kids, I don't think vice principals do that much."

"You're right, but it would be good for the kids. The current vice principal is pushing seventy."

Well, that settled that. "Come on," I helped her up before scooping up the binder on her desk that she kept looking at with a panicked expression.

"What are we doing?"

"We're giving this work back to who it belongs to. Where is her office?"

"I don't know if I can do that, Ryan."

"We aren't being rude, but you aren't doing more work when you're already stressed out. It isn't good for you or the baby."

We walked to the principal's office only to find it empty. Lights out, guess someone likes to go home on time. Even Reese seemed perturbed by the idea that she was expected to stay late, yet the one handing off her work left promptly half an hour after school hours.

I reached for a sticky note behind the front desk and wrote out a note for Reese.

Unable to help out with this project due to it being Thanksgiving break. In the future, I would not like to be considered for extra projects and research as it is not in my job description. -Reese

"I can't just leave a sticky note."

"What's she going to do? Tell on you for not doing her job?"

"I just don't want it to be awkward between us."

"It will be a little awkward, but she has to learn not to step all over you. What if she does this after the baby is born, and you have to wait hours to get home and miss out on important things for our kid?"

That sobered her up quickly, she rested her hand on her bump that was hidden by a thick sweater and nodded confidently.

"Now, let's get home, I ordered takeout from Nick's to celebrate the start of Thanksgiving break. And I took the dogs back home, so we can have some peace and quiet."

Chapter 14

Reese

I pulled my chunky cardigan closer around my midsection for the hundredth time in the fifteen minutes that we'd been in the car. My mother's house was on the complete opposite side of Rosewood to my apartment building, and I was grateful for the extra time to mentally prepare. Quiet filled the car, and the energy could only be described as the calm before the storm.

This would be the time I usually gave my boyfriend's 'the talk' about my mom. That was the only reason I had ever brought anyone home before, so this was uncharted territory. Thankfully, Ryan was well aware of my mom's situation, and I could save my breath. He had celebrated quite a few Thanksgivings at the Finch household over the years when his mother flew the coop or forgot to prepare a meal. My knee still bounced rapidly at the thought of telling our parents I was pregnant.

I turned to Ryan to find him gripping the steering wheel so tight his knuckles were white. "Are you nervous to tell your mom?"

He shook his head quickly. "No, are you?"

"A little," I admitted. "But I'm excited to see your mom's reaction, I feel like she'll be excited."

Ryan's mom was constantly in motion. She started harassing him about getting a girlfriend when he was in eighth grade, I remembered vividly because I was her first choice in a 'future daughter in law'. I used to admire her love for love. There was always a new man around their house, and if there was no man, then Teresa Summers wasn't at home. She would leave for weeks at a time on romantic getaways only for the relationship to not work out a week later.

Needless to say, we had no need to worry about Ryan's family, his sister was a sweetheart and would be supportive as well. She went out of her way to come home from her last semester of college to do this impromptu family get together between our two families. I just couldn't help but worry my mom would ruin the mood.

"We'll be fine," Ryan assured. I wasn't sure if he was talking to me or himself.

We pulled into the drive, and Ryan parked the car. I made no move to get out, and to my right, he seemed just as glued to the seat as I did. To give him motivation, I reached for his hand and squeezed it reassuringly with a smile. Fake it till you make it right?

Our calm was interrupted by screeching from across the street. In the decade or so since Ryan and I had been out of our parents' houses, they still remained neighbors. Which was a blessing and a curse, my mother never left her house, so Ryan's mom was often her only source of town gossip. Every time I got a call, I was being asked about Ryan or if I had heard from him.

"Reese!" Teresa screamed in my ear as she pulled me into a welcoming hug the second I exited the car.

"Hey, Ms. Summers, how have you been?"

"Oh, please, call me Terry. How many times do I need to remind you?" She pulled back from the hug to hold my elbows and gaze into my face with a big smile. "I'm very excited to hear what this Thanksgiving is all about. I expect there is so much to be thankful for this year!"

I laughed softly while Ryan intercepted her embrace to give his mom a side hug. Ryan's sister, Jenny, strolled up behind her mother to greet us as well. Neither of the Summers siblings seemed to have inherited the fireball energy of their mother. She gave me a small smile and hugged me quickly before cringing at her mother clinging onto Ryan for dear life.

"I'm so proud of you dear, you had me worried, but you turned it all around," his mother said, bursting with excitement while holding both sides of his face.

He gently pulled her hands off of him and nonchalantly asked, "What exactly is it you're proud of?"

She turned to look at me, then Jenny, before covering her mouth to attempt to hide a very girlish giggle. "Oh, nothing dear, I'll play along."

Inside, my mother was cooking up a storm, likely out of anxiety. I definitely inherited that from my mom, but we let out our anxious energy in different ways. She barely gave me a side glance before pointing at the cake on the counter.

"They gave me the wrong brand, whoever they let pick out groceries to be delivered needs to look for other work," she grumbled. "Don't go blaming me if it tastes off."

I smiled before giving her a kiss on the cheek. "I'm sure it will taste wonderful, Mom."

127

"And you keep your distance too, who knows what you catch from all those kids at school."

"Yes, ma'am." I found the pile of plates and silverware she had picked out for today and went to set the table. The house wasn't small, but the amount of over-sized furniture in it made every room feel that way. I guessed when it was just my mother here, it made her feel less alone.

"Oh, Josephine, it smells just heavenly in here." Terry's voice echoed from the kitchen to where I was busy in the dining room.

Ryan appeared soon after in the doorway. "You aren't supposed to leave me," he muttered. He grabbed place settings and helped to set the opposite side of the table from where I was standing.

"I was just helping, that's all," I assured.

Three hours later, we were all sitting around the giant walnut table. Hand in hand we said a prayer, I didn't think any of us were actually religious, but my mother often did things for show. We all let go and started passing plates of food piled high, there was enough to feed a small village.

I felt Ryan's foot tapping me throughout the meal. When I looked over to him to see what was up, he looked white as a sheet. His head nod suggested he wanted to get it over with and tell everyone, but I wasn't going to announce our unplanned baby right as Teresa was finishing up her story about falling in love with three different men in Greece over her week-long vacation this summer.

Finally, the conversation came to a lull, and I took the opportunity. Ryan and I naturally agreed that I should break the news, because he wasn't the best with words, and I was best at placating people if the reaction was bad. My hand absentmindedly rubbed my stomach over my dress as I cleared my throat.

"So, I'm sure you've all been wondering why we're doing Thanksgiving together this year since it's been a while," I said. Teresa went so far as to drop her fork to listen better. "Ryan and I wanted to share with you all that we're having a baby together."

No better way to break the news than to drop it like a ten ton wrecking ball right on the Thanksgiving table. The silence could suffocate anyone. Under the table, Ryan found my knee and gave it a reassuring squeeze while we waited to find out our fate. Jenny was the first to offer us mercy.

"No way, I knew you would always end up together, but a *baby*," she enthused. "I'm going to be an aunt!"

I leaned over to my left to give her an awkward hug around the table. "You'll be a wonderful aunt."

Terry's silence was scaring me. I didn't know if I had ever heard her silent in the entire time I had known her. Which was quite a long time. I peeked over at her to gauge how bad it was, only to find her quietly sobbing. Her head was down, and literal tears fell into her mashed potatoes.

"This is so wonderful, I expected good news but this," she paused to suck snot back into her nose. "This is the best news. I am so grateful."

Two for three. The third would never give in so easily, though. I decided beforehand that if my mother waited for everyone to leave and then went into a spiral, that would be considered a win. The look on her face told me that was unlikely. She stared right at me, almost through me, with her hand clenched around a fork that was sunk into a piece of turkey.

"Pregnant," she whispered.

I suddenly realized this wasn't a one-way conversation, and that I should explain further. The anticipation of everyone's reactions made me forget the whole speech I had planned. I needed to reassure them there was nothing to worry about, explain our plan, and bring everyone together. It was a lot to ask of one small speech.

"I realize this is very sudden for everyone. We are a little shocked ourselves, but we want you all to know that we're both very excited and on the same page about this baby," I said confidently.

Opening statement done, acknowledge their stress and worries, and soothe it over with confidence and positivity. I was about to march right into my next sentence when my mother stopped me.

"Are you getting married?" she asked.

Was it rude to ask people to save their questions for the end? It worked in teaching, so it was my natural instinct, and that was not a question I was ready to answer just yet. "No," I grimaced.

My mom gasped in shock and horror. Her little girl, having a baby out of wedlock and following in her same footsteps. I imagined this was her worst nightmare since she reminded me constantly throughout my life that hers stopped the second I was born. Maybe she would feel a little satisfaction in knowing I would get what was coming to me finally.

"Well I think this is just lovely, no one should go running headfirst into a marriage anyway," Terry said. "Besides, we know how it turned out for us." Her finger pointed back and forth between herself and my mom and I thought I saw my mother's head explode. "You two will be just fine."

I watched the woman who raised me as her face turned red, from embarrassment or anger, I wasn't sure. My mind raced to find all of the preplanned answers and defenses I had, yet I drew a blank. There wasn't much to do other than watch her panic and wait for it to be redirected back to me.

"So are you moving in together? I just can't get over you two, what a beautiful couple," Terry's oblivious joy filled the room. "Love is so wonderful, it looks great on you both. You're going to make each other so happy."

My chest tightened at the realization I would now have to explain that not only are we not getting married, but we weren't even in a relationship. Then we would have two non understanding mothers on our hands.

"Well-"

"Yes, we're looking at houses now. We just haven't found the perfect one yet," Ryan answered for me. He cheaped out by taking the easy question.

"Also," I started again.

Ryan squeezed my hand under the table, a signal I could only translate to mean 'shut the hell up'. "It's going well, though. We hope to be in a house before Christmas."

"Well I'll be!" Terry clasped her hands together with a giant smile. "Your first Christmas as a family. I better get a Christmas card."

I looked to Ryan to see if he was going to correct her. With Mom still stewing across from us, I wasn't too opposed to going along with the assumption we were in a relationship. We *were* having a baby together, why should they need to worry over the fine details when they knew all of the major facts.

"Yeah, there's definitely a lot to be thankful for this year," I replied cheerily. The smile on my face was genuine, *tense*, but real. I hadn't realized how much weight I was holding on my shoulders keeping this a secret.

* * *

"I'll come visit soon, Mom, love you," I said quietly before kissing her cheek.

She grimaced and nodded, "Yes dear, please do."

Her energy resembled someone who had just got done attending a funeral rather than a family get together or finding out she was going to be a grandmother. I realized a long time ago, I couldn't take my mom's worries personally. If there was nothing left to worry about, she would always come up with something.

We walked back to Ryan's car and sat down. He cranked the keys and immediately turned down the radio as it filled the car with sound. I didn't even know where to start, so I sat in silence mulling over everything that happened in my own head.

"Well that went well," he said.

I couldn't help but laugh. "Could've been worse."

The rest of the drive was in silence. I had no idea how Ryan felt, but I felt free. My mother was disappointed and clearly not excited over me having a baby, but I was still breathing. The world was still turning.

"I never want our holiday's to be like that. With our kid, I mean."

"Agreed." He wrapped his arm around the back of my headrest. "My mom is hardly ever in town for them, so that takes care of one half of the situation."

"Mine hates having people over, so I don't think she would

mind," I added. She would complain, of course, if I didn't offer. Usually though, she refused to see anyone else other than me or Ryan's family since she'd known them for so long. Even they weren't allowed sometimes.

"I don't want to just cut them off though," I corrected. "Maybe we could just do a separate holiday with them. And have our own with just our family."

"Meaning you and me?"

"Oh- I just meant-"

"I know what you meant, Reese. We are a family, you're right."

I read a quote a while back that said you have to disappoint your parents if you want to live a happy life. That couldn't be more true in my case, and I was happy to be doing this with Ryan. Even if we weren't in a relationship, he always had my back, no matter the situation, and the important ones especially.

14

Ryan

The nearest hospital to where we lived in Rosewood was about a twenty-minute drive. Reese sat next to me, squeezing my hand nervously while she talked away about everything and nothing. It was something she did to calm her nerves, so I was content to listen to her talk. My usual playlist had done nothing to distract either of us anyway.

"It's nice to see someone else do all of this, isn't it?" Reese said.

I hummed. "Like a practice run, almost."

She laughed at my logic. It was honest though, I had to pave my own way my entire life. I was the oldest sibling, with no father figure. My mother, who was around sometimes, was more of a live-in camp counselor rather than a parent. My sister and I had probably helped her out of problems more than she ever helped either of us.

This felt like an entirely new feat. I could take care of myself, it was the one thing I had done no matter what, because the only way I could help my sister and mom was if I was stable enough to lend a hand. No one else mattered much, until Reese got pregnant. She changed everything.

Now, I had not only Reese, but a baby to take care of. And I had a feeling that giving out money like I did with my family wouldn't please Reese in the slightest, especially if house hunting was anything to go off of. I had no clue what the fuck I was doing. So it was nice to be able to copy off of Ashton's notes.

The smell of rubbery hospital soap filled my nose as I washed up. Reese was checking in on Georgia, and I did my best to avert my gaze elsewhere. If Reese looked as worn out as Georgia did right now, I was going to freak out. It was one thing to hear how hard being pregnant and giving birth would be for her, but to see Georgia after birth put it all into perspective.

Her normally tanned skin and rosy cheeks were stark white, and her forehead was clammy. She looked like she had just seen death and came out of the other side. The only consolation was the giant smile on her face. She clearly hadn't regretted anything. Would Reese regret going through all of this for me and our baby?

"She looks *just* like you!" Reese emphasized for the third time.

She stood next to Georgia's hospital bed, slowly swaying back and forth with the tiny baby. I peeked over her shoulder and couldn't discern any features that looked like Georgia or Ashton. She was just 100% baby to me. Reese turned her body to face me when she noticed me lingering.

"Do you want to hold her?" Georgia asked.

"Oh, no, I'm okay, Reese seems to be doing a good enough job," I said. I grimaced slightly at the thought of doing something wrong and making the kid cry. "How are you doing?"

"I'm alive, just relieved this little girl is here," she said wistfully. Her hand lifted to rest against the bundle in Reese's arms. "I think the anticipation of giving birth was scarier than the real thing. Don't listen to all of the horror stories, there's no need to freak yourself out."

The last part was directed toward Reese. She nodded and said, "I'll have to tell my mother to shut her trap."

Laughter filled the room as Ashton walked in with food and a giant water cup for Georgia. I added that to my mental list of things to do while Reese was in the hospital.

"Hey, you two," Ash greeted.

Reese looked up to greet him with a smile, "Two little girls, you're one lucky man."

"I know," he said, his smile blinding. "I couldn't have asked for anything more."

He walked over and clapped me on the back. "Good to see you too, man. Haven't seen you in a while."

"Seeing as you're preparing for a new baby, that's probably a good thing. You're busy."

"Have you ever held a baby before?" he asked.

Not this again. "I'm sure I have at some point in my life."

I watched Reese's eyes widen at the slight confession. "You've never held a baby? Here, sit," she gestured. "Hold your

135

arms in a cradle like I'm doing."

I sighed, knowing there was no argument to get out of this. I sat on the couch before positioning my arms as she had hers. At least there was no way to drop the baby like this, now I just had to hope she didn't burst out crying at the sight of me.

"The most important thing is to support her neck, so put your hand under her head like this," she started to hand her off and I panicked. My back was ramrod straight as I focused on holding the baby properly. "Good, just like that!"

Reese backed up when she felt I had a good handle, and I felt all of my muscles clench. I could not relax. The baby squirmed a little, and I couldn't help but admire how cute she was. She may not look like anyone, but she did look adorable as hell. I hoped our baby was cute.

After about three minutes of tensing every muscle in my body, I was saved by the bell. Or a nurse to be exact. She needed to take the baby off to be tested, another thing I took note of. Ashton decided to go with them and dragged me along with him.

"So, how are you feeling?" he asked.

"You're the one that just had another kid. How are you feeling?"

He laughed. "Don't deflect the question, I can see the wheels spinning in your head."

"I'm fine, I'm guessing Georgia mentioned that we're having a baby. Reese will be a great mother," I said confidently. The other half of this equation was definitely the problem. "How did you juggle volleyball and a baby when Ruth was first born?"

Ashton had Ruth, his first baby, about six years ago. The relationship with her mother didn't work out, and she essentially dumped Ruth in Ash's lap to take care of. There was a short window where he was co-parenting before he eventually retired from his career to take care of Ruth on his own. I would make the same choice if it came down to it, but I still needed to make money, and I wasn't keen on giving up the one thing I was good at.

"It's hard," he admitted. "Really hard, but you and Reese have been through a lot together. You just have to communicate really well."

He reached over to mess up my hair. "Which might be a hard chore for you. You can't be stubborn though, nothing will humble you like a kid."

I nodded. Reese had said something similar, but what the hell was communication going to do when we had no plan. We were just friends doing our best to make a happy life for a child. There was no blueprint, no guide for what to do after the baby was born, it was just up to us. I tasted blood in my mouth before I even knew I was gnawing the shit out of the inside of my cheek.

"You just have to be there," Ashton said quietly. The humor in his tone was gone. "Every chance you get, you be there for them. It's the little things, getting up late at night, helping out with chores, sharing meals, that's what matters."

"Yeah," I mumbled. "I'm guessing it sounds easier than it is."

"It is," he agreed. "But you have Reese to do it with, so it's not like you'll be miserable, pal."

I rolled my eyes. We were back to our usual antics, and I couldn't help but wonder how much longer everyone would keep up with the Ryan and Reese jokes when they realized she didn't want to be in a relationship with me. It was only a matter of time.

* * *

Waking up to muffled bangs, I sat up with urgency. I heard clamoring from the kitchen and went to investigate. The front door wasn't open, so it seemed unlikely someone broke in. What I found was a half asleep and frustrated looking Reese standing in front of the stove.

"What are you doing?" I grumbled.

She jumped a little and clutched her stomach. "What did I say about sneaking up on me?"

"Well technically you're the one being sneaky, what's going on?"

She huffed. "I want fried rice."

"Is this a craving?" I asked. I was surprised I hadn't been asked to make any late night grocery store runs so far.

Her head bobbed up and down.

I looked over at the clock, it was two in the morning. The advice from Ashton earlier ringing in my ears, I decided, "I'll make it. Go lay in bed, and I'll bring it to you."

"You won't make it right," she admitted guiltily. She stared into the pot of boiling white rice helplessly. "I won't even make it right. Have you ever had Nick's fried rice? That's what I want."

"Okay," I pondered. "How does he make it?"

"I don't know," Reese whined. "He does something weird with the eggs, I think. I have a wok, I just don't know what to do."

"Alright, you go back to bed. I'll take care of it," I repeated.

"Ryan-"

"Just trust me, I'll make it Nick's way." I pressed my hand to her lower back to turn her around and guide her back to her room. "It'll just be a bit."

When I got back in the kitchen, I pulled out my phone and prayed to anyone out there who might listen. Dialing Nick's number, I leaned back against the counter and watched the rice boil.

"Hey," he greeted quietly.

"Hey, I know it's the middle of the night, but I have an emergency only you can solve."

"It's fine man, we're up just watching a movie. What's up?"

"How the fuck do you make fried rice," I demanded. "And I don't need the general way, I need to know how you specifically make it."

He laughed into the phone. "I can't imagine what got you in this situation."

"Just start with the instructions, chef. I've already got plain white rice boiling."

Chapter 15

Reese

I pulled up Zillow for the third time in the past hour. My desperation caused me to expand my search limits to twenty miles outside of Rosewood, in hopes that the perfect house would magically pop up in my feed. It still hadn't. It's not like we were on a time crunch, there was no rush to get a house. Definitely no ticking time bomb growing in my stomach.

Ryan walked in, presumably back from the gym. He always looked so good all sweaty after a workout, it took all my self preservation not to jump on him. His biceps especially made me want to sink my teeth into them, and the sleeveless tanks that were completely inappropriate for winter didn't help my urges.

I blamed it on the pregnancy hormones.

"Hey, did you make breakfast yet?" he asked.

My sexual urges died with the snap of my laptop. "Why do you assume I would just make breakfast for the both of us?"

"Reese, I-" he said, suddenly on high alert. His hands were both up to appease me.

"Seriously, the one thing I give you ownership of, you haven't even attempted to do. Did you know I'm three and a half months pregnant now? That's, like, almost halfway! We don't even have a suitable living environment for our baby, that's literally the most basic step."

"Honey," Ryan cooed. "I'm working on it. I understand the stress you're under, and I'm taking care of it."

"Working on it is just not good enough, Ryan." I sat back on the futon and crossed my arms before putting my feet up on the coffee table. I'm pretty sure I had seen literal toddlers take this exact position in an argument.

"Alright," he sighed. "Put on a coat."

"I don't want to go house hunting again, you said you'd take care of it. If you're giving up, I'll take over, but I'm not going to go tour a bunch of houses outside of our price range."

He walked over to the coat closet and grabbed my coat anyway. I was wearing sweatpants, which were one of the only comfy pants left after my bump began growing, and one of his long sleeved t-shirts. I couldn't leave the house like this.

"It's a quick drive, come on."

Too annoyed to continue arguing, and a little curious, I gave in. After shoving my sock clad feet into warm boots, we both headed to his car. He drove in silence, nothing but the quiet sounds of his decade old playlist filling the air.

When I noticed he was driving toward our parents' neighborhood, I felt nothing but dread. I was about to tell him to take me back home when he pulled into a familiar driveway a street before I expected. This house was on a corner lot of two residential streets, one of which being our childhood street. I knew the lot well because this was our bus stop for the entire time we were in school. It was about a ten minute walk since we had to travel all the way from the back of our

141

neighborhood out to this corner. I would never forget waiting here in the freezing cold during winter.

"What are we doing here?" I asked.

Ryan looked at me from the corner of his eye. "You don't recognize it?"

"Of course I do, this is our old bus stop."

"You like this house," he added.

I leaned forward in my seat to look up at the beautiful two story home with a shingled roof and beautiful pale green siding. Ivy trailed up the front of the house from the garden bed filled with various bushes and seasonal flowers. It was my dream house as a kid. I imagined that, since the yard and outside of the house was so pretty, if we lived there my mom would love going outside.

"It's a beautiful house, but it's not for sale." My eyebrows pulled together as I waited for his explanation. Maybe he was more hopeless at being able to buy a house for us than I originally thought.

He reached into his pocket to pull out a keyring with three gold keys on it. "It's not for sale because it's ours."

I froze. My mouth closed and opened a couple of times like a fish as I gathered my thoughts. "What do you mean?"

"This house," he waved his hand toward the stunning home in front of us. "It's ours."

This had to be a prank. "I don't believe you."

"Let's go in then," he insisted. He jumped out of the car to wrap around and open my door. I hadn't moved since I was convinced this was all a joke and some annoyed old couple would come out to scream at us any second.

"This isn't our house," I said.

He paused in helping me up. "You don't like it?" he asked.

"No!" I blurted out. "No, I mean I *do* like it. I just meant it's not possible this is ours, I haven't seen it on any home listed sites. And we would have seen the for sale sign when we drove by here a few weeks ago."

"Just come on, Reese." He helped me out of the car, and I cautiously walked up the front steps. There was no welcome mat. Just pretty ivy and an abandoned plant pot on the porch decorated the outside.

Ryan pulled out his keys and looked closely to find the one he wanted. When he had it picked out, he shoved it into the lock and turned it to open the door. The doorknob twisted and I was waiting for a production crew to come out with cameras and a boom stick.

None of that happened, though. He just opened the door to an empty house, and I followed closely behind him inside. I was speechless as I swiveled my head to find endless wood floors and white walls. As far as the eye can see.

"I wanted to wait to show you until it was a little more ready. I thought the emptiness would stress you out, but I didn't realize how much you were worried about having a home until this morning," he explained. "The power and gas aren't hooked up yet, they're coming later today."

"When did you do all of this?" I wondered, more to myself than to him.

"What do you think I do when you're at work all day?" he joked. "It took a while to figure out, but my mom apparently dated the owner's brother-in-law. Long story short- he only uses this house in the summertime. So he was open to selling it when I asked."

I turned around in a full circle, still admiring the open layout of the first floor. This was the feeling that I was looking for when I toured all of those other houses, my mind filled in all the blanks. That blank wall over the fireplace would be filled with pictures, we had the perfect amount of room for a bench and shoe storage by the front door. I kept turning, and more ideas flooded my head as I stopped at a tree.

"The Christmas tree places were starting to sell out, so I figured I should get one now. I know you love the smell of the real trees."

I spun toward Ryan with tears in my eyes. Wrapping my arms around him tight, I knew everything was going to be okay. He had done all of this, just for *me*. Well, and our baby. But also for me. This was my dream house, my favorite kind of Christmas tree, my *home*.

I sniffled into his shoulder while Ryan laughed at my sappiness. Little did he know, he was the biggest sap in the room today.

"I'm so sorry for doubting you," I said into his damp shoulder.

He chuckled lowly, "It's okay, I'll find a way to forgive you." He pulled back to look at my tear stricken face and gently brushed the tears away with his thumbs. "And for the record, I didn't expect you to make me breakfast, I was asking to see if you had eaten yet. I wanted to go to Nick's."

"I'm sorry," I said again. I shoved my face back in his shoulder to hide my embarrassment.

His arms wrapped around me to rub my back soothingly. It was clear I was drastically off base with all of my assumptions, this whole time I thought he hadn't even *tried* to look for a house. Meanwhile he had gone and bought one all on his own.

"What about the money? I still want to pay you back my share."

"We can talk about that later, we should get you back home,

it's freezing in here." He shrugged off his coat to wrap it around me on top of mine.

It was chilly, only slightly warmer than outside. My feet were firmly planted, and I wasn't leaving this house anytime soon. He had only just shown me the place, and now he expected me to skedaddle? No chance.

"No, I want the full tour," I said cheerily. The warmth in my heart would make up for the chill in the air.

He wore an expression that I couldn't read and offered his elbow to me. "Right this way."

* * *

We sat, sprawled out on the hardwood of the giant living room. A bare Christmas tree stood in the corner leaning against the wall, while Ryan and I were sitting right in the center with sunlight from the giant windows streaming down on us.

"I really think my entire apartment could fit in just this room," I admitted.

"It's almost half the square footage," Ryan mused. I looked at him to gauge if he was joking, he was not. "I was thinking that we could go furniture shopping later this week if you're feeling up for it?"

I gasped. "Of course, that will be so much fun!"

"We don't have to do all of it in store, I don't want you to push yourself too much."

"I'll be just fine." I looked over to catch him looking at my stomach. "Do you want to feel? She's not kicking or anything yet, but you can still say hello."

He nodded, seeming uncertain. I unzipped my coat before grabbing his hand and pushing it to my bump gently. He looked up at my face.

"Should I talk to it or is that weird?"

I laughed airily. "Of course you can. And stop calling our baby an It."

He leaned in to speak closer to my bump, "Hello, baby. Just wanted to check in to see if you're doing well." He glared at me as I held in a laugh. "I'll give you a tour of this house too when you're ready, I hope you'll like it."

"Do you think our child is your future boss? This is the most professional I've ever heard you speak."

"I'll have to practice more before they get here," he mumbled grumpily. I knew he wasn't actually upset from his eyes crinkling at the corners when he sat up to look at me again.

"You can practice anytime you want," I agreed.

Chapter 16

Ryan

I opened up the take out boxes delivered to us from Nick's diner, to push the one with a blueberry muffin and eggs closer to Reese. My actions were halted by the sight of Reese in tears. Just seconds ago she was laughing and joking with me, what did I do wrong now?

"Are you okay?" I asked with all the caution of speaking to a wild animal.

She nodded sniffily, "I'm just so relieved we have a home."

My heart clenched painfully. "Reese, did you really think I would let us be homeless or live in that closet much longer? Of course we have a home."

She laughed a little at my exasperated tone. It worried me that she seriously doubted my ability to complete the one task she allowed me to do on my own since we started this. Sure, I sometimes took care of our meals or did our laundry, but buying a house was the only big thing she had trusted me with during this journey. I wasn't going to fuck it up.

I watched her lingering hesitation before moving our food out of the way. We were both still on the living room floor of our soon to be home, since she refused to leave. I reached forward to grab onto my coat that was wrapped around her, over her own, and slid her closer to me. The hardwood floor made it an easy feat.

When she was right in front of me, I grabbed her elbows and waited for her to look directly at me. I wanted her to really hear me, and I was sure I would have to say this a thousand more times, but I would continue if I needed to. Her eyes flicked up to meet mine, her face poking out of three layers of hooded jackets.

I started speaking before I could lose my train of thought, "I'm not going to half ass any of this, because I know you're depending on me. We said we're doing this together, so you don't have to do anything alone. It's not all resting on your shoulders, even though I know you think it is, just like you think everything does. It doesn't."

"I'm lucky to be having a baby with you," she said, smiling through her tears. How could anyone not fall in love at the sight and sound of that? She was perfect, and I was willing to keep proving I was worthy of calling her mine. I was definitely all hers.

To avoid ruining the moment, I just pinched her cheek and shoved food in her hands. She needed to eat, and I needed time to process what that sentence meant, and if it meant I had any chance at what I was really hoping for. But I wasn't willing to risk ruining this perfectly happy, yet icy, day over asking her to remind me of our friendship status.

A few hours later, we were supplied with warm air and lights. Reese took off my coat to fashion it into a makeshift pillow to sit on while we played cards. She still refused every attempt at getting her back to her apartment so far, which I took as a sign that she really did love the house. I was secretly content to stay too, even though this hardwood floor was killing my back, there was a lightness in the air. It felt like everything would be okay, nothing to worry over, and if we took one step out of that door it could all come crashing down.

"So have you thought of any names yet?" Reese asked. Most likely to distract me from the fact that I was winning our current game.

I blew out a breath. "I was thinking Jack if it's a boy."

"Have you seriously not thought about it at all," she asked while laughing.

"I have," I said with a straight face.

She lightly pushed my shoulder as I won. We laid down our cards, and Reese stood up to walk around and stare out the windows. "You only said Jack because we're playing cards."

"Yes, but that isn't the first time I've thought of it," I insisted. It was true, my mind often wandered to baby names. It was a clear showing of what kind of parent you would be. Every person I met now, I judged them on whether or not their parents made a good call or not.

Jack ticked off all my boxes– correction, my one box; it wasn't the name of anyone I disliked. I had no idea how many names I had a negative connotation with until I considered naming my own child.

"What if it's a girl?" Reese trailed her way back to stand in front of me now. "Let me guess, we'll name her Queen," she said teasingly.

I stood to be closer to her. "I thought that was already decided." I pushed back her long sleeved t-shirt to reveal her one and only tattoo, a lily, on her arm.

"Oh, Lily?" She looked dumbfounded. "I actually hadn't

thought of that."

"I think it's a nice name," I pondered.

"It's beautiful," she replied, looking a little misty eyed again. "I'm still not convinced you didn't just look around the room for the first objects you saw." She laughed wetly at her own joke.

I couldn't help but roll my eyes. "You're such a sap," I said dryly.

"It's overwhelming to think about all of the memories we will have here," Reese whispered. She continued walking from room to room as she spoke, "Holidays, dinner parties, birthdays, and all the firsts our baby will have. First steps, first meal," she spun around excitedly. "First word! She better say mama first."

I chuckled. "So we're sure she's a girl now?"

"I just like the name Lily. I'd be happy with either, though," she chirped.

I walked closer out of instinct more than anything. I was the moth to her flame. She looked so happy, genuinely happy, and I couldn't help myself. There was no uncertainty in her eyes either, all she did was smile wider when I pushed my hand into her hair and brushed the apple of her cheek with my thumb. Reese, *my* Reese, was perfect. It was impossible to ignore when I was halfway across the globe, and it sure as hell was impossible now.

I hesitated, remembering her boundary about just being friends. My hand pulled back and fell at my side, but I couldn't bring myself to step away.

Her hands came up to wrap around my midsection, pulling us closer. One of her hands grabbed mine and guided it back to her cheek. Her back arched to continue looking up at me, and I wished so badly that I had done this sooner.

"You care about me," she whispered fondly.

I quirked an eyebrow. "You're just now figuring that out? Only took a little over a decade, I suppose," I muttered to the side of her face.

She pulled back more with wide eyes. "Don't act surprised, Finch. It's obvious."

She blinked a few more times before responding, "You care about me." Her voice had less dreamy undertones and sounded more like 'oh shit'.

I watched her process the statement and look away, only to look back at me a few times before she seemed to make a decision. With her leverage on my shirt, she pulled me closer and pushed up on her toes to kiss me. *Holy shit.*

Chapter 17

Reese

I was sick of denying how much I wanted him. My mind raced as I kissed him. My best friend, my- what the hell do I call him now? I couldn't think of any reason as to why we shouldn't make each other feel good. Kissing him felt great, and he cared about me, he bought a house for me, we had already done this before.

Everything was working out well so far. I let him take care of finding us a home, and he actually followed through. The sky didn't fall, and I didn't have to save the day.

I was suddenly lifted off the ground with Ryan's hands under my ass. Instinctually, I wrapped my legs around his waist and chased his lips again. I wanted him, I had wanted him ever since that night around the bonfire. He wasn't just some person I could have a fling with and forget about it, he was *Ryan*. Every piece of him he gave me only made me want more.

He walked us up the stairs to what I assumed was the main bedroom, what could be our bedroom. Once there, he pushed off my coat and threw it on the floor before gently laying me down on top of it. His giant hands moved under my shirt and pushed up over my boobs.

His feverish kisses trailed from my lips to my jaw and down my neck. I grabbed handfuls of his shirt and helped him pull it over his head. All I wanted was to feel him against me. His body against mine, without all these damn clothes in the way.

Once he got fed up with groping me through my bra, he shoved my shirt up too and unclasped it smoothly with one hand. I gasped at the feeling of the sudden chilly air against my nipples, and he watched them harden. His eyes were dark, and I waited anxiously for him to touch me again.

His hands reached for me first, pulling me to sit up and into his lap. Ryan's warm hands now trailed up my bare back, rubbing to keep me warm while his head bowed to take a hard nipple into his mouth. The contrast between the cold air and his hot, wet, mouth made me let out a gasp.

He took his sweet time between the two of them, and in the process made me desperate for more. I wanted that tongue in other places. His hands continued rubbing mindlessly up and down my back until I pushed his shoulder a little for him to let up.

"I want more," I said breathlessly.

He kissed me with slightly swollen lips before laying me back down on my coat on the floor. "What do you want, Reese?"

I froze. What did I want? What did he want? I was being greedy, he spent all this time making me feel good, and here I go asking for even more without even considering-

"Stop thinking so much," he said. He pushed his forehead to rest against mine. His body hovering over me was enough to keep me plenty warm and happy. "What do you want more of?"

I breathed shallowly while trying to form words. He had

an uncanny ability to make my brain stop functioning, and I was embarrassed more than anything. He bought this whole house for me, and I was already asking for more. It was so unlike me.

My mind stopped when I felt his mouth return to my nipple, and he only continued to kiss lower. He followed a path down my stomach and was met with the waistband of my sweatpants. When he saw me watching him, he hooked two fingers into the sides and slowly pulled them down. I lifted my hips a little to help him.

"This what you wanted?" he growled.

I nodded quickly. "Yes, please."

He pulled me back into a kiss as his hands rubbed up and down my thighs. I couldn't help but grind into his lap, too turned on to be patient. His kisses were slow, too slow. I reached for his big hand resting on my thigh and pushed it into my panties.

"Need you, Ryan. Please," I whined in his ear.

His groan in response sounded tortured. His thumb found my clit and rubbed in slow circles while my hips kept moving on his lap. I could feel he was hard beneath me, but he still kept his restrained composure.

I pulled back slightly to rest my forehead against his cheek, so I could catch my breath. Quiet moans escaped me as he kissed another path down my neck with his hand still in my panties. Two of his big fingers pushed inside of me, and I pushed my face in his chest.

"Oh fuck," I cried.

"Relax, baby." He pushed my thighs further apart with his hand that wasn't inside of me. "I can barely move."

His fingers curled deeper inside of me, hitting my sweet

spot and stretching out my pussy. I could only cling onto his shoulders for dear life. My hips had a mind of their own as I started riding his fingers to reach my release faster.

His hot wet mouth on my neck and his free hand playing with my nipple nearly sent me over the edge. His whole body focused directly on me as he continued rubbing my clit in deliberate circles with his thumb while his pointer and middle fingers stretched out my cunt. Sounds poured out of my mouth that I had no control over.

"Are you gonna cum for me, baby?"

I nodded wordlessly, my eyes shut and focused on the feeling building in my lower abdomen. "Feels so good," I whispered.

His moan in my ear was what sent me over the edge. He sounded so wrecked, even though he was the one pleasuring me. He bit my earlobe and pulled gently while my legs started shaking.

"Fuck, I'm gonna-" Words escaped me as my entire body flooded with an overwhelming feeling. I had never come so hard in my entire life.

The hand that was on my tit moved up to brush back my hair. "You okay, sweetheart?"

All I could do was let out a mumbled hum, my face still shoved in the crook of his neck and shoulder. My body felt like jello, and I selfishly took a few seconds to relish in the feeling. His hard on in his pants was what brought me to look up at him.

"Your turn," I said breathlessly while rubbing him through his jeans.

He kissed my nose and gently pulled my hand away from his pants. "I'm good. Come 'ere."

He scooped me up sideways and held me in his lap. His

naked chest felt great against my side, and I couldn't help but feel pangs of guilt.

"I want you to feel good, too."

"I don't do that with friends, baby," he said into my ear. I started to sit up and explain my sudden change of heart, but he stopped me. He kissed my hair and continued tracing mindless circles on my thigh. "Trust me, that was just as good for me as it was you. Let's just relax for a minute."

The serotonin flooding my brain must have taken over, because I agreed happily. I just wanted to sit here with him in our pretty new house, all warm and cozy. My arms wrapped around his waist, and I sunk impossibly deeper in his chest to cuddle with him.

The comfortable seat that was Ryan's lap must have lulled me to sleep. I woke up to him lowering me into the passenger seat of his car. Somehow he had dressed me without waking me up, and I was grateful for the puffy coat wrapped around me to fight off the biting cold of the outside air.

"Sorry," I said sheepishly.

"Don't be, baby. Let's get you home."

He walked around the car to get into his side and started the car. "Thank you for taking care of me."

"Always." He rested his hand on my thigh. "If you ever need me to do that again, just let me know."

I blushed at the implication that he would give me orgasms whenever I wanted. The nagging feeling at the back of my mind told me this could complicate things later, but right now I just wanted to focus on the nice warm hand on my thigh and the man next to me that made me feel like I was floating.

We got back to my apartment and took off our coats in comforting silence. Usually, I would be freaking out about the events that just occurred, but I wanted to just relax and have a nice day. I walked toward my bedroom before pausing in my doorway.

"Do you want to sleep in here tonight?" I asked. He looked at me like a deer in headlights. "Just as friends, I mean to sleep. I think it'd be nice to sleep next to each other."

He tilted his head and considered my offer. "Okay, do you want to talk about earlier?"

"Not really, no." I looked up at him with uncertainty. "If you want to, we can. Right now, I just want to lay down with you."

He gave me a slight smile and his eyes looked a little sad. "Let's lay down together, then."

I started second guessing my decisions, but his hands on my hips again stopped me. He led me to the bed and waited for me to climb in. Once I had, he slid in behind me, his chest pressed against my back. The warmth was delicious, and I found my eyelids slowly closing again.

Chapter 18

Ryan

Everything was coming together, we officially had a house, the baby was doing well, Reese let me take care of her. Something had to complicate it. I ignored more calls from my manager over the last couple of weeks than I could count. My focus was needed here, with Reese and our baby. I told myself once we had the house figured out, then I could worry about my job.

I was sitting on Reese's futon, home alone while she was out helping put together Christmas presents for some family she knew through school. I had ignored the call of duty for too long, it was time to figure out how this would work. My phone rang three times before I picked it up.

"Hey, man," I answered reluctantly.

"Summers, wherever the hell you've been, I hope you've been training."

"Every day," I sighed.

"Well, as much as I appreciate your self sufficiency, I'd like to get you back in the gym with Julian." My long term trainer, Julian, wasn't bad, but the gym we used was about an hour and

158

a half from Rosewood. Not a fun drive.

"I can see if I can fit a few days a week into my schedule."

"Look, kid. The Olympics will be here before you know it, and we still have to get you on that team. There's a training camp in February, we need to have you ready for it."

"Where is it?"

"The training camp will be in New York, are you hearing me though? That's only a couple of months to get you to your peak."

"Yeah, I'm listening. How long is the training camp?"

"Three weeks."

Fucking hell. Three weeks was a long time to be away from Reese when she would be six months pregnant and all alone. I hated the idea of it, but I also needed a job to provide for my family.

"Ryan, you there?"

"Yes, still here," I grunted. "I'll talk to Julian about scheduling time together."

"Perfect, early bird catches the worm. Talk soon, kid."

I decided to keep packing, having my hands busy always helped me think through problems. Packing up books from Reese's shelves would have to occupy my mind for now. There were boxes placed randomly throughout the apartment, thankfully there wasn't much stuff in here to pack. My goal was to get us out of here and in our home in a week.

Reese interrupted my packing a couple of hours later with a quiet thud of the door shutting. She walked in with a smile on her face and her hands filled with cookies.

"Mrs. Rainsy made these for us, she heard we bought a home. Isn't that nice?"

I had no clue who Mrs. Rainsy is, but I grabbed a sugar

cookie and stuffed it in my mouth anyway. "Yeah, she seems great."

"Wow, you've gotten a lot done." She set down her things and looked at the somewhat organized boxes I had stacked up against the wall. "Thank you, I feel bad for making you do most of the work."

"Don't, you're growing our baby," I said. I leaned down to give her a quick kiss on the cheek as a greeting, sugar still stuck to my lips from the cookie. "You're doing the bulk of the work here."

We still hadn't officially decided what we were, but I figured between the baby and the house, my intentions were obvious. Reese seemed happy, and I found myself wondering why I ever worried about us working out. There was a real chance we would end up together as more than just friends. I could be the one to make her happy, despite all else.

The ball was in her court now, if she wanted to throw out our friendship bracelets and upgrade, it was up to her to say so. I was happy to be patient, I'd spent years knowing I wouldn't be worthy of her in my wildest dreams. If there was any inkling of a chance, I would wait for it.

A nagging feeling creeped into my mind as I watched her fill up her water bottle and sit down on our futon. Then she smiled at me, and it was gone nearly instantaneously. This would work, I came back to Rosewood to feel like myself again, spend time with people I loved. I just had no idea I would get that wish tenfold.

I joined Reese on the couch and pulled her feet into my lap. "Are you still up for furniture shopping today?"

She nodded excitedly. I watched her stare at her sock covered feet before asking, "Do they hurt? I know it's still early, but they're supposed to swell up right?"

"They're a little sore, I think it's just from walking a lot lately," she said sheepishly.

Wordlessly, I started massaging her ankles before gently putting pressure on the soles of her feet and rubbing them in circles. Foot massages weren't my specialty, but I would figure it out if that's what she needed me to do. I looked back up to find her watching me with confusion in her eyes.

She had always been awful at asking for help, and a little too good at offering it. I used to think it was ironic that we were opposites, but maybe it was less ironic and more perfect. Reese was easy for me to read. I knew when she needed something. In the past, I let her work it out on her own. I was never one to go out of my way to offer help if someone didn't ask for it. I could change for her, though.

I watched her relax into the little green decorative pillow she always kept on the futon and fall asleep. We still had plenty of time in the day, and I figured we could be more productive shopping if she got in a nap first. My Google searches told me women tire a lot more easily when pregnant. I was also never one to turn down a mid-day siesta.

A nudge to my shoulder brought me back to the land of the living. "Ryan, we have to go shopping, we fell asleep," Reese whispered.

"Okay, give me a second," I grumbled. Despite sleeping in a real bed for the first time in a while the night before, my muscles desperately needed a good stretch.

We both fumbled our way through stretching and sliding our shoes on to head out the door. I grabbed a few of the boxes I'd packed earlier to drop off at our house on the way to the furniture store. The goal of the trip was to find large furniture pieces that we needed in order to move in. Or, at the very least, get an idea of what we liked and didn't like so we could find what we wanted online.

* * *

"Where should we start?" Reese asked, staring at the sea of furniture and displays in front of us. It felt a little daunting to be honest.

I looked to my left and found rows upon rows of dining tables and chairs. "How about there?"

She led the way, and we were off. It took about two tables for me to realize I had practically no opinion on types of woods or table legs. On the third table, Reese seemed really excited about the six seater table with rounded edges. I picked up on her pleased tone and agreed immediately. As long as the thing had four legs I would be satisfied.

The same process happened through stools, side tables, bed frames, you name it. Until we found my one passion, couches. I would be damned if we got anything that couldn't fit an entire volleyball team on. Hopefully, I would never need to sleep on it again, but if I did, I would make damn sure I could lay with my legs fully straightened.

Reese pointed to a leather couch that was slightly bigger than the futon in her apartment now. "This one is cute, let's see if it's comfy." I watched her sit down on it and bounce up and down a little.

"It's nice, but it's too small. You have to keep in mind how big that living room is, remember?" And how long my damn legs are.

She seemed surprised at my negative comment. "Oh, okay,

which ones do you like?"

I looked around and found the biggest in the room. It was a few couches over from us, so I helped Reese up and we walked over together. I stood in front of it happily. The thing was giant, it was an L-shaped couch with deep cushions, and enough room for two of me to lay flat.

I turned to Reese to see what she thought. She stared at it like she was doing her best to find one redeeming quality about the thing. The thing looked like a damn cloud, so I sat and pulled her to take the seat next to me.

She seemed to change her mind after sitting down. "This is really comfy!"

We leaned back, her feet nearly coming off the ground to get her back far enough to rest against the cushion. It was damn comfortable. And while I could see it might not be the prettiest couch, I was willing to beg her to let me have it anyway.

"Do you like it?" I asked hopefully.

She nodded her head with a laugh. "Yes, but you love it." My face must be as easy to read as hers is.

"I'm considering buying two."

She only laughed harder and leaned her head on my shoulder. "I'm willing to compromise on one," she offered.

"Deal," I blurted. *No fucking take backs.*

We took a few minutes to enjoy the comfort of a good couch (one I wasn't sure Reese had ever experienced before if hers was any indication). So far, we had ticked off most of our list apart from baby furniture. I decided that room would need its own dedicated shopping trip, this was overwhelming enough as is.

"Do you actually like the furniture we picked out so far?" Reese blurted out unexpectedly.

Shocked, I turned to her. "Yeah, why?"

"You really seem to love this couch, so I'm just realizing I might have steamrolled over you up until now." She looked guilty, and I couldn't help but put my hand on her thigh to stop her.

"I love it all, even that giant barrel for a side table you picked out."

Her mouth formed a small circle. "You don't like the side table? It's not a *barrel*, it's just circular."

"Yeah, it's great. Reminds me of a pirate ship or something."

"You hate it!" she said loudly. "Why didn't you say anything?"

"I don't hate it," I defended. "To be honest, I can't tell the difference between most of the stuff in here. It's all just slightly different colors and shapes. So I trust your sense of style."

After a pause I added, "Except the barrel, that thing belongs in a museum."

She gasped before shoving my hand off her leg jokingly. Her arms crossed over her chest, and I couldn't help but look at her tits all pushed up in her shirt. "I told you I was unsure about it anyway, we can pick something else out."

"No, no, we're getting it now." I stood up and scanned the barcode on the couch with the scanner the store staff gave us. "Let's go check out, unless you want to look at anything else?"

"I don't think we'll be able to fit anything else in the house with this couch in it. So we'll have to be done," she said sassily. I looked down to hide my embarrassing smile as I followed her to the registers.

We were setting up a time slot for the furniture to be delivered directly to the house when my dreams came crashing down. "Unfortunately sir, the couch can't be delivered with the rest of your furniture. It's store policy."

"Okay, I assume we can just order it online then?"

"No, this model is no longer sold online, only in stores," he said unhelpfully.

"So, we can only get it if we pick it up." I repeated.

He nodded and looked at his computer awkwardly while I mourned. There was no way that couch could fit in either of our cars, even if it broke down to a dozen different pieces. I'd just find a similar one somewhere else.

"That's fine. Can we pay for it with everything else though and pick it up over the weekend?" Reese chimed in.

I looked at her like she had grown another head. "That won't fit in my car, and it's not worth it to rent a truck."

"We'll just get Ashton to help, it's no problem," she said.

So I finally found a loophole in Reese's 'never ask for help' mantra. If someone needed help that she couldn't provide, it must circumvent the entire rule. I guarantee if it was any of the furniture she picked out, she never would've asked Ash.

"Sounds good," I agreed. Getting help from Ashton wasn't something I would normally do, but I could also put aside my morals for this couch.

Seconds later, I heard an affirmative beep. My head shot down to see Reese tapping her card on the card reader. I stared at her incredulously, not wanting to make her feel awkward in front of the person helping us.

We confirmed the delivery date and were on our way. The second we were in the parking lot I barked, "I was going to pay for that. I'll pay you back."

"No, since you bought the house, and you keep dodging me when I ask how much you paid for it. The least I could do is pay for the furniture inside the house."

I opened the passenger side door for her grumpily. She sat

and stared up at me innocently. When she made no move to buckle herself, I reached into the car and pulled it across her chest to buckle it for her.

While I was still in her space, I pushed hair out of her eyes and insisted, "I'll pay you back. We make very different salaries, and you didn't have time to plan for this."

Her head tilted cutely, and she bit her lip. "I like doing this together, so I don't want it to be all one-sided. So far it's just been me demanding stuff and you buying it. That's not how I want this to go."

Compromise. She was so hell bent on paying for half the house in the beginning, and never letting me take care of her. She adjusted her rules for me, and I could meet her in the middle on this one thing. I'd pay for all of our bills soon anyway, so she would make it up over time.

I stood up straight and rested my hand on the car door. "Okay, you can pay for the furniture. That seems fair enough to me."

She smiled up at me happily, and I decided that I'd made the right decision. "I don't want you going broke though, so if it's too much you let me know," I said.

Her eyes rolled. "You act like I have no money whatsoever," she teased. She paused and then corrected, "I mean my apartment is pretty bad, but that was mostly out of convenience."

"Uh huh," I agreed sarcastically. "Hands and feet in the car, please."

She shifted her body to be fully in the car before I closed the door for her and got in on my side. I turned on the heat immediately because I knew she liked to be nice and warm. My phone rang, and I checked it to find my manager calling once again, ignoring it, I started the car.

"Do you think our parents were this hopeful before they had us?" Reese asked.

Not something I thought about often. "Maybe. I don't think they were as prepared as we are though."

I glanced over at her to see a slight pout on her lips as she pondered. Her father left her mom before she was even born, so clearly he wasn't too hopeful. Mine left soon after I turned two. Our mothers weren't perfect people either, but who was?

"I just want to do better, you know?" she asked quietly.

I nodded silently. If anyone could be the perfect parent, it was her. My contribution to the equation was the only input that was questionable.

"We'll do better," I assured her.

It honestly would be hard to do worse, my mother was absent a lot of my childhood. Emotionally, she had always been a friend or roommate rather than a parent. I couldn't remember a time when she treated me like a kid rather than someone to listen to her problems. When we got older, her list of revolving boyfriends kept her away on sleepovers and vacations, all while my sister and I were home fending for ourselves until she got back.

Reese's mom wasn't much better. She was borderline agoraphobic, as long as I knew her, I had never seen her mother leave the house. I didn't really know if she had always been that way, or if it got worse over time, but it left a lot of responsibilities to fall on Reese. I remembered seeing her carrying home groceries in middle school each week and eventually joined in on her weekly trips sometimes in high school.

My phone ringing again stopped my thoughts of the past. Reese spoke over the melody, "You can answer it, I don't mind."

I glanced at the screen to see it was my manager again. "It's nothing, I'll call him back later."

I hung up, only for the ringtone to start up again thirty seconds later. I let out a long sigh before answering it. My car was already connected to Bluetooth, so it played on my speakers, and I didn't have time to switch it off before Mark dove headfirst into the conversation.

"Don't you ever check your phone, kid? I emailed you the contract for that training camp. Need you to sign it ASAP."

I rubbed my temple to soothe my annoyance. "Will do, I'm busy."

"Training, I hope. I also spoke to Julian and he said he hasn't heard from you yet, you need to book that time now. I mean it, you need to get back in the gym or you'll blow this."

"I'll do it. There's a lot going on right now."

"Soon, all you'll have time to have 'going on' is volleyball, so take care of whatever it is." Muffled noise filled the air from his end of the line. "Go sign that contract now. It's electronic, you can use your phone from whatever hole in the wall you're hiding out in."

"Got it, goodbye." I huffed, annoyed as hell.

Tension singed the air after I hung up. Pulling into the parking lot of the apartment building, I turned off the car and unbuckled my seatbelt. I caught Reese looking at me nervously before doing the same and getting out of the car.

We walked side by side into the building. "So, you have a training camp? Is it for the Olympics?"

"It's the camp to prove why they should choose me for the Olympics. Sort of like tryouts. I just found out this morning." The elevator jumped to a start as we headed to our floor. "It's going to be three weeks long."

168

"Oh," she replied.

"It's not until February, so we have plenty of time to figure out everything for the baby before I have to leave."

She nodded and gave me her best fake smile. Anyone else would have fallen for it. "Yeah, that's exciting. Everything is all coming together, you must be so happy."

I gave her a small nod, but I certainly didn't feel happy at that moment in time.

Chapter 19

Reese

Moving days get a bad rep. Every time I've moved into a new place in the past has always been a monumental step forward, maybe it was because I grew up in the same house my entire childhood. So today was shaping up to be pretty sweet in my book.

Ryan was already out and about, he rented a box truck to move his belongings from his assigned athletic housing in the city. It was a few hours drive, and I offered to go with him, but of course he declined. As my bump started to grow, he only seemed to get more protective over me exerting myself. I found it cute, if anything, that he thought being pregnant would slow me down. I had things to do.

I got out of bed and managed to get ready in my new bare essentials apartment. Only the big stuff was left, Ryan refused to let me help him carry furniture, which I couldn't disagree on too much. The baby came first, and I wanted to be careful.

The first knock on my door turned out to be the Reid brothers. I let them in and they started lifting my furniture like it was made of marshmallows. Escorting them downstairs,

170

I did the hard job of opening doors for them.

By the time Ryan arrived with the truck of his belongings, we had the last of my stuff sitting in the parking lot waiting. I watched him jump down from the driver's side door. He greeted me with a small smile before turning to open the back of the box truck. It revealed dozens of boxes, and I was hit with a wave of reality. We were really doing this, officially moving in together.

Ryan stepped back to stand next to me, and three angry red lines on his forearm caught my attention. I grabbed his arm and pulled it closer. "What happened to you?"

He sighed before chuckling at the question. "I figured you wouldn't want to leave your cat friends here, so this morning I brought them and their houses to our house."

"You what?"

He raised his eyebrows. "Was that a bad idea?"

"For your arm, apparently." I looked to the back of the parking lot where the cat houses normally were. "You captured cats? Did you at least get it on video for me to watch?"

"Watch it, old lady. Anyway, they're at the house for you. I put them in the garage for now, so they wouldn't run away and get lost."

My heart skipped a beat at the thought of him waking up at five in the morning just to capture a very feisty group of cats for me. I gave him a quick hug and turned to catch Ashton and Nick exchanging a look.

Will got out of the passenger side of the box truck and joined us near my furniture. "Alright, lady and losers, are we ready to get this show on the road?" asked Ashton.

"Ready!" I called cheerfully. As they started loading up the furniture, I remembered this was it. My last opportunity to

171

say goodbye to my home for the last few years, and I decided I needed to take it. "I'm just going to do one last sweep to make sure we didn't forget anything inside while you guys move this."

"Want me to help you?" Ryan asked over the top of the dresser he was lifting with Nick.

I shook my head and turned around to head inside. "Just don't leave without me."

"Wouldn't dream of it," he scoffed.

My mind was so occupied with everything else going on, I hadn't realized how I might feel saying goodbye. Nearly every aspect of my life changed in a matter of just a few months. Even though I was happy, and especially excited to become a mother, I still felt like I needed to mourn my old life. The days of spending sunrise to sunset with friends, working, or volunteering were over. I had to put my family first.

It was scary, the idea that I would spend so much time inside my house caring for a baby, at least for the first few months after they were born. The ingrained fear of becoming my mother made me want to revolt against that. However, there wasn't much you could do outside of your home with a newborn baby.

I had Ryan though, so everything would be okay. If I needed fresh air to reset my mind he could take care of the baby for a few hours. I just hoped he wouldn't be gone too much for volleyball, and I could never ask him to take days away from training. Mr. Olympics most likely wasn't too forgiving of athletes taking time off.

My legs carried me throughout every room of the apartment as I quietly said goodbye. Farewell to my shower that couldn't stay warm longer than three and a half minutes. See you never, to the wall that my neighbors slam their headboard against every night. Good riddance, to that small window that barely let in any light.

I patted the wall next to the front door one final time before switching off the light switch. "It was wonderful staying with you, take care."

And with that, I made my way home. Our makeshift fleet of vehicles piled into the driveway of my beautiful new house. It still felt unreal that it was ours, I wish I could go back in time and tell teenager Reese that she was living in this house with Ryan and having a *baby*. I'm certain she would have passed out from shock.

"Ash and I are going to take his truck to pick up the couch while you guys start with the rental if that's okay." Ryan already looked stressed about the day ahead.

"Yeah, sounds good, we can take care of this," I assured.

He gave me a look before pointedly looking at Nick and Will. "Don't let her lift anything heavier than fifteen pounds, she's sneaky, so keep an eye on her."

"I'm not a child," I defended as I crossed my arms in a very non-childlike way.

"No, but you're stubborn as hell."

"Just go get your couch, will you?" He laughed at my sassy tone and gave me a quick side hug before hopping in Ashton's truck.

Clay pulled in my driveway with a couple of his friends I recognized soon after Ryan left. I knew Ryan would be too petty to ask him to help us move, but we needed all the hands we could get to move our stuff along with the new furniture that was being delivered later. I let the men move the furniture from my apartment inside before I started grabbing small boxes.

Doing my best to set boxes in the rooms where the items inside belonged, I quickly realized everyone else was placing furniture and boxes with no rhyme or reason. We could always go back and move things later, I reasoned with myself.

Then I nearly tripped over a box as I walked in the front door. Why the hell would someone put that right in the pathway of everything else, especially when we would be moving big furniture pieces through there. I set my box down to the side to pick up the intrusion and brought it to the right room. Then I continued on my mission of putting my costume box in the closet when I heard a loud crash.

I hurried down the stairs. "What happened?"

"Sorry, we must have stacked the boxes too high," one of Clay's friends said sheepishly.

He stood next to four large boxes toppled over across the living room floor. "It's fine, no worries. I can take care of it."

He nodded and went back to keep grabbing things from the truck. I looked around to make sure no one was nearby before loudly sighing. It was just an accident, no problem. I got to work on fixing his mistake and found the box that he had stacked on top was filled with my books and incredibly heavy. I did my best to flip it upright and slide it out everyone's way.

The next box had silverware and plates in it, and I sighed again. These were the only plates we had to my knowledge, so if they were broken, it was another thing I needed to add to my to do list to go shopping for. I moved it out of the way as well, only to watch Clay walk in to set another giant box right in the entrance to the living room.

I sat on the floor and did my best to control my frustration.

Everyone was so kind to help us, I couldn't micromanage them and order them to move boxes my way. That was just silly. They were doing this out of the kindness of their own hearts.

I started shoving the last box from the stack that fell over, out of the way, when out of the corner of my eye I saw Will walk in and nearly face plant over the box that Clay had just set down. He caught himself and let out a grunt before putting the side table he was carrying down next to the boxes I had shoved out of everyone's way.

"You need help with these?" he asked.

"No," I said quietly. "All good." I was sure the smile on my face did nothing to convince him. I was officially pissed.

I stood up and followed Will toward our entryway to move the box he tripped over. I turned it on its side to find it was bath towels. In one big lift, I picked it up to find it a lot heavier than I expected bath towels to be.

Trudging up the stairs to my bedroom (Ryan and I played rock paper scissors for the main and I lost), I let out deep breaths with every step to get up there. I was really struggling, and while I didn't work out much, I wouldn't consider myself weak. On the last couple of steps, I tripped a little and stubbed my toe while dropping the box. Thankfully, I fell upward and it landed on the top step.

"Hey," Will yelled. "You okay?"

"Fine." My voice filled with annoyance. "Just tripped a little."

"Hold on a second." He started walking up the steps and gently grabbed my elbow to help me upright before reaching around me to push the box out of my way.

We both managed to get on the landing and he reached down to carry it for me. "Where are we putting this? It feels pretty heavy, you should probably stick with the lighter stuff."

"The bathroom." I felt defeated, and a frog found its way into my throat. From the look on his face, I knew Will could see the tears building up in my eyes. "It says it's supposed to just be bath towels."

He silently brought it to the bathroom in my new bedroom and ripped it open with his bare hands. We both peered in to find it filled with other bathroom supplies, like shampoos and conditioner along with towels.

"That would be why it's so heavy," he deadpanned.

I nodded and sniffled, doing my best to avoid looking in the mirror. He stood awkwardly and waited for me to get my shit together. I tried my best to remember that positive attitude I had this morning, but it was impossible to find within me.

"Are you okay?" he asked cautiously.

I sniffled again and tried to manage my emotions by myself. "There's just so many boxes everywhere!" I blurted out.

"They're all just putting them in the middle of where we're walking, that's so dangerous! I watched you trip, you could've gotten hurt. And I don't know what I'm going to do with all this stuff, they aren't even labeled properly," I gestured to the box next to us.

"How am I going to raise a baby in an empty house filled with boxes! They're not even in the right rooms, they're just thrown everywhere and anywhere. My plates are probably broken because Dan or Jim or *whatever his name is* stacked books on top of them and let them fall over. I don't want to have to buy more plates, I already have all of Ryan's things to find places for, all of our new things we've bought, and an entire house to put together."

I took a giant breath, realizing I hadn't taken one in a while. Will looked as if I had just brought him a pile of dog poop and left it at his door. I knew he didn't want to deal with this, so I did my best to swipe the tears out from under my eyes and fix it myself.

"It's fine, sorry I just needed to rant a little. I realize I'm being ridiculous."

"No," he said quietly. "I get it, it's a lot." He looked around the room in search of answers. "Come on, let's go downstairs."

He offered me his elbow to grab onto as we walked down the stairs only to find another pile of boxes waiting for us in the entryway. Nick was on his way inside with two more and Will turned to me before I could physically combust from frustration.

"Reese, why don't you go in the kitchen for a minute while I talk to Nick."

Grateful for a minute to myself, I listened and went to stand alone in my empty kitchen.

I heard Will quietly talking to Nick as I walked down the hall, "Unless you want our very kind and very *pregnant* friend to burst into tears, I need you to listen to me."

Turning into the kitchen, I bent over to hold my head in my hands and rest my elbows on the counter. Will was wrong, I was going to burst into tears no matter what. I was so excited for today to happen, how did it all go wrong? There was no need for me to be so upset, usually I would just brush something like this off and fix it myself after everyone left.

I gave myself thirty seconds to ugly cry. I covered my mouth with my shirt to muffle the pathetic noises, I was crying over absolutely nothing. And the fact I couldn't control the crying only made me cry more. Humiliated, I covered my face with my sleeve covered hands to dry my tears and took a deep breath.

Will came into the room when I was counting my breaths to calm myself down. He looked a little like he was being sent to the gallows, but then again, his face always sort of looked like that. He set down the box labeled silverware and plates on the counter gently.

"They're going to start putting the boxes in the right rooms." He crossed his arms and did his best to look anywhere but my face. "I think it would be a good idea to start unboxing the kitchen."

"Oh, but the rental truck," I said sheepishly. "I get why you guys are just unpacking it, we have to return it before the end of the day."

He turned his back to me to start opening the box of, fingers-crossed, plates. "They can still unpack it in time, they were just being lazy assholes."

Will was always a very straightforward person when asked a question. It made me wince a little, but it was nice to know he always meant what he said. I was a little embarrassed about my outburst earlier, and debated begging him not to tell anyone else. He had clearly at least hinted at it to Nick.

"Okay, I can do this alone then. I'm sorry for being so ridiculous."

"You aren't being ridiculous, Reese." He started taking out dish towels that I had wrapped around our plates. "This is a two man job, here let me go grab you a chair."

Great, I had a babysitter. I tried not to focus on my embarrassment and instead the excitement of finally unpacking, this was the part I was excited for. There was something so magical about starting fresh and picking out the perfect place for everything to go. It was the act of creating a home, and I wanted to make the best home for my baby.

Will reappeared with one of the chairs I used at my small breakfast table in my apartment. "I'm really okay to stand."

"Just humor me, Reese." It sounded less like a question and more like a demand. Not wanting to ruffle any more feathers today, I sat down and waited for him to hand me a box. He didn't. "Alright, so it looks like we got lucky, they're not broken."

He held up the set of six intact plates. "Any idea where you want these to go yet?"

"Maybe in that cabinet next to the microwave?"

He opened the one I was referring to. "Bottom shelf?"

"Yeah, I think that's good." I squirmed a little in my seat. "Do you really want me to just... sit here?"

"You're not just sitting there," he pointed out, looking over his shoulder at me while his hands collected forks and spoons. "We're getting rid of these damn boxes. And you're the only one of us who knows where everything should go, so this is your job."

"Alright." I turned to greet Nick as he dropped off two more boxes for us and grimaced. This felt a little humiliating watching everyone around me do the job that I was supposed to be doing.

Boxes kept appearing, but Will and I were quick with organizing. Every time we emptied a box, he broke it down and threw it out in our garage with the cats, and for that I was grateful. Eventually, he let me help unbox the glasses and mugs since there were a lot of paper towels and bubble wrap to protect them. He made sure to prop the box up on another box, so I could continue sitting on my chair while I worked.

I felt a little silly still, but as we continued working, my frustration disappeared. We mostly worked in silence except when he asked my opinion, "Do you think mugs should go on the bottom or middle?"

"Hmm, I think the bottom since we use them a lot, but maybe on the left hand side and then glasses can go on the side closest to the fridge?"

He hummed in agreement. "Which glasses do you use most?"

"I think these taller ones," I held one up for him to see. "And the wine glasses can go up top since I won't be using those for a while."

Loud voices carried through the hall into the kitchen and a lot of commotion followed. My heart rate spiked, but I decided it was best to stay in my chair in case something went horribly wrong. I wasn't sure I could control my emotions if I walked out to find a hole in the wall or something.

Will peeked his head out, but seemed to decide it wasn't worth his time. We continued organizing cups until Ryan walked through the doorway. He looked out of breath and overworked, and I felt even more guilty about my breakdown over stupid boxes.

"Hey, how are we doing in here?" he said with all the caution of a person walking on icy sidewalk. Nick had clearly given Ryan a heads up on my meltdown.

Will answered for me. "We're good, just getting the kitchen put together."

"Yeah, we make a good team," I said honestly. I hoped there weren't still tear stains on my shirt and my eyes had gotten less puffy.

Ryan's eyebrows raised a little. Will and I were an odd duo, out of all of our friends, he was probably the last person I would have expected to help calm me down in a crisis. He did a pretty good job though.

"Good, I realized you probably haven't eaten yet. We stopped by the diner and I grabbed a muffin for you." He handed me a paper bag. "And in case you aren't in the mood for a muffin, there's ice cream in the freezer."

"Ice cream for breakfast?"

He put his hand on the counter and leaned toward me with light dancing in his eyes. "I've seen you eat ice cream in the AMs plenty of times, no judgment here."

Chapter 20

Ryan

I was only gone for a couple of hours and these bunch of knuckleheads managed to make my pregnant future wife cry. Nick insisted it was everyone's fault, but I blamed Clay. I couldn't believe she even invited him here in the first place, did she not think I was capable of taking care of everything? We didn't need that asshole to help us move.

The rest of the guys, including Clay, carried my couch inside while I paced for a minute and thought about what to do. She was clearly overwhelmed with all of this, apparently she put a ban on bringing boxes inside unless they were organized properly. I needed to get this truck emptied in the next hour though so we had room in the driveway for our furniture delivery.

When I had my answer, I stormed in to find her in the kitchen with Will. At first glance, she seemed perfectly fine to me. Her cheeks were a little pink upon further notice, and my fist clenched at the thought of her crying without me being there to comfort her. I wasn't sure what part Will played in all of this, but she seemed to be happy with him.

I greeted them both and gave Reese her breakfast. Her voice seemed genuinely happy, but I still needed to know what went down, so I asked Will to come help with something in order to get answers.

"Oh, and Charlotte's here. Do you want me to grab her, so she can come help you?" I directed at Reese.

She perked up at the mention of her friend. "Yeah, that would be great!"

I found Charlotte in the living room with Nick and asked her to keep Reese company. Once we were outside, I turned to interrogate my friend.

"What happened? Nick said Reese was crying."

"She's okay now."

I waited for him to continue. When it was clear he wasn't going to, I asked again. "So what happened?"

"She just got frustrated with the guys leaving boxes everywhere, which is fair. They were being idiots and leaving them in the walkways."

It was very unlike Reese to let people know she was frustrated. So if she got to the point where she told Will that, it had to be pretty bad. I couldn't picture her being upset over just boxes though, it had to be deeper than that. Right now I didn't have time to talk it out with her, and didn't want to embarrass her by doing that with a bunch of our friends in the other room.

I walked back through the house and passed everyone taking a break on my brand new couch on my way to Reese. Their asses would get a reprimand next. I needed to make sure Reese was okay first.

"Hey, do you mind if Reese and I talk alone for a minute?"

"Of course, I'll just be out there," Charlotte answered.

183

"Will told you I acted like a big baby huh?" she said while looking at the floor.

I pushed a strand of hair that fell in front of her eyes behind her ear. "No, he said the boys were being idiots and made you frustrated."

"No, they really didn't do anything wrong." Her puppy dog eyes nearly made me melt. "I don't know why I got upset, I guess I just freaked out when I realized all the work we have to do. We just have so much stuff, and we don't even have anything for the baby yet. I want this to be their perfect home, and I can see it being that, but it's going to take a lot to get there."

I nodded and started breaking down an empty box for her. "Moving is stressful, I'm sorry I wasn't here to help."

"It's okay, honestly Will helped a lot." She let out a cute giggle. "He didn't really talk, he just quietly organized things with me. It was weirdly calming."

I laughed and pressed my thumb between my eyebrows at the image of Will silently panicking and stacking cereal bowls while Reese sat on her chair ordering him around. It was a strange method to calm her down, but whatever works. I made a mental note to thank him later, and another one to try it myself if the opportunity ever came up.

"I'm glad it helped, how do you feel about getting out of here for a little bit while we finish unloading the truck?"

"I can still help with the lighter boxes."

"I know, but we'll have a lot of unpacking to do later. What if you went with Charlotte to go buy those plants you were talking about."

She looked down at her hands. "I feel bad for making everyone else do my job, I haven't helped much."

"We have a whole house worth of boxes for you to help with when you get back, Reesey piece. Trust me, you'll get your opportunity to help." I grabbed her hands so she would look at me. "You said you want the house to feel like a home, plants will help right?"

She nodded slowly. "I feel like such a schmuck."

I couldn't help but snort. "You're not a schmuck." I reached up to tug at her ear playfully. "And if you are, you're *my* schmuck, so suck it up and go get us some pretty plants, buttercup."

"I'm definitely going to kill them."

"We'll just keep buying more, you'll learn eventually."

She let out a wet laugh, and I wiped the lone tear trailing down her cheek. "You're so nice to me," she said sappily. I nearly broke on the spot. This was a long day though, and I needed to stay focused on getting this house in order.

"You deserve it all, and more." Clearly I wasn't doing a good enough job of supporting her with everything that happened today. She really did deserve more.

* * *

"Thanks for helping out, I really appreciate it." I shook Clay's hand and squeezed as hard as I could. What did Reese ever see in this guy?

"Are you sure you don't want more help? You still have about a quarter of that truck out there," he said. I was well aware.

"Yeah, we've got enough of us now, just needed help while Ash and I went to go pick up our couch."

"Alright, if you change your mind just let me know."

"Will do, here, lunch is on me." I put a bill in his hand. I hated the feeling of knowing he had something over me. Giving him money wouldn't fix that, but it helped a little.

"You don't have to do that," he said. "We're friends, I just wanted to help out."

"I know, just take it. Go save some more cats or something." My joke fell a little flat, and we said goodbye before he loaded up his two buddies and was on his way.

I walked back inside to take a seat on my couch. Around me Nick, Ash, and Will all stared at me like I was crazy. Maybe I was, but I hated the idea of Reese's ex helping us move into our home that we were going to raise our baby in. Even if we could be friendly, that was too much.

"Can we just knock the rest of this out please?" I asked.

* * *

All four of us were collapsed on my couch by the time Charlotte and Reese got back. I was right when I said it could fit nearly an entire volleyball team, and thankfully the unpacked boxes in front of us made for the perfect coffee table for us to eat off of. I swallowed my last bite of orange chicken before standing and gesturing for Reese to take my place. Charlotte had already sat next to her fiance and grabbed a fork.

"Wait, no plants?" I mumbled through gulps of cold water, handing a fresh water bottle to Reese on my way back to the couch.

She smiled happily. "Plenty of plants, they're just in the car."

"There are a couple we might need a hand with," Charlotte added. Her fork was perfectly poised to steal from her fiance's plate when he wasn't looking.

"I'll go grab them then." I made my way out to Reese's car and noticed her following closely behind me. "You seem much happier now," I muttered as I pulled her into my side for a quick, and very sweaty, hug.

"You're getting your sweat all over me!" she accused while laughing. "And yeah, I think I just needed some fresh air. I got us a doormat too, should we put it out?"

"Yeah, go ahead while I grab this." I had no idea how Reese or Charlotte or whatever poor attendant that was helping them managed to fit an entire tree in her car, but they had. Reaching for the pot, I did my best to bring it out of the car carefully.

It took a couple more trips of me carrying plants inside to notice the doormat. "Oh, this is nice," I said to Reese who was beside me holding a couple of smaller plants in her hands. The doormat said 'Welcome Home' in cursive font with snowflakes in the corners.

I felt less tired, and more proud after seeing that. We were building a home together, and today was the first day of that, of course it was going to be a little stressful. The important thing was that we both felt it was all worth it in the end.

"Should we do a show and tell while you guys eat?" Reese sat on the edge of the couch, giddy at the prospect of showing all of her friends the plants that were sitting right in front of us.

"Go ahead," Ashton said through a mouthful of food. "I think we have some of these in our house, that one is Georgia's favorite," he pointed to a smaller plant with white and green leaves.

The endearment in his voice caught me off guard. Did I talk about Reese like that? And more importantly, did she talk about me like that? I had never heard her speak about me with that much fondness, but Ashton and Georgia were married with her at home with their newborn baby. Hopefully we would get there.

"Alright, so this one is going to go in the living room by this giant window because it needs the most sun. I thought it would look nice on that barrel side table you love Ryan," she talked at the speed of an auctioneer.

I couldn't help but relax back and admire her. Every single thing she bought had a specific spot in her mind, a reason for why she liked it, and a unique trait that made that plant different from the others. She put more thought into buying plants than I put into my entire life. So much of it happened by chance, and I just went with the flow.

Her cheerful show was brought to a close with the tree I helped carry for her. "Is this one going to be our new Christmas tree?" I looked over at the still undecorated tree in the corner of the room. "Don't like that one enough?"

She scoffed at my silly joke. "No, this will go in the baby's room. It's a fiddle leaf fig, they grow much bigger, and I thought it would be cute to take pictures of the baby next to it. So we can see a side by side of both of them growing up together."

That was so fucking sweet, only Reese could come up with it. My throat tightened up, and I began to wonder if I was allergic to orange chicken and had forgotten.

Charlotte said what I couldn't while beaming up at her friend, "I think that's a lovely idea."

I nodded and muttered my own agreement. Somehow I needed to keep up with this beautiful angel of a woman, when I had done nothing but look out for my own skin my whole life. She was so thoughtful, and I felt the doubt set in that I was a little in over my head.

Chapter 21

Reese

In the midst of all the unpacking we were doing, I had totally forgotten Christmas. Neither Ryan or I were very religious, but growing up, my mom and I had always celebrated for fun more than anything. And I wanted my baby to have those same magical memories of waking up Christmas morning to presents.

Our cat neighbors strolled up to me as I got out of my car. They were much friendlier, ever since we relocated them to living in our backyard. Stumbling inside my front door, I took a moment to appreciate our new house. I did this every time I came or left the house, and I wasn't stopping anytime soon. It was especially wonderful with the furniture we picked out together, and a few art pieces and posters we had before moving that seemed to work together somehow.

Once in the kitchen, I planted my shopping bags on the island and shrugged off my coat to sit down. The larger this bump got, the easier I got out of breath. It felt a little like a weight was on my chest, and we weren't even halfway through this pregnancy yet.

Ryan was away in the city working with his professional trainer. Since his training camp for the Olympics was coming up, he was spending every day he could with his trainer to prepare. I was proud of him, but it was a little lonely since I had work off and most people were away traveling or spending time with their families.

That was part of the reason I decided to decorate for Christmas on Christmas Eve Eve, not an official holiday, but I liked to think it was. These decorations wouldn't be up for long, but I thought it was important as our first holiday here together to go all out. Even if the baby was still in my belly, he or she could sense how lame or cool we were, and I wanted to impress them.

It would also be a nice surprise for Ryan to come home to. He was a little distant lately, I knew something was bothering him, but he refused to tell me what it was. His act of pretending would have fooled anyone else, but not me. I was beginning to worry he was regretting moving so fast.

Moving in together on a whim was one thing, but having a baby together was a whole other life-long adventure. I hoped I didn't bulldoze him into making this decision. I thought I made it clear in the beginning that him resenting me was my worst nightmare, and every day that nightmare seemed a little more like a potential reality.

Sure, we were sleeping under the same roof, having most meals together, and spending time together unpacking. He was off, though. And that wasn't something I could get over without fixing it first.

Hopefully a little Christmas cheer would do him some good. He wasn't exactly the holiday-loving type, but who could be closed off and grumpy in front of a beautifully lit tree and stockings?

"Reese, did an elf break into our home or something?" He turned the corner to find me in the living room sitting on a pillow on the floor.

I grabbed the box and hid it behind my back as quickly as I could. "Wait! Go back into the hallway."

He gave me a look, like I was being ridiculous, but followed suit anyway. "Don't you know you're supposed to announce your arrival home?" I called. "You could have seen your present!"

"I thought we were just doing small presents this year," he spoke through the wall.

"We are," I agreed. My lips pouted while I focused on finishing wrapping quickly, but also keeping the lines nice and neat. "How was training?"

"Good." There it was. Everything was good, or fine, and nothing was wrong. It was beginning to drive me crazy, but I didn't want to ruin the magical effect of our newly decorated home.

"Okay, you can come out now." He peeked his head into the living room to make sure the coast was clear before joining me in front of the tree.

"You did all of this on your own?" I smiled proudly at him and nodded. He wrapped his arm around my waist and pulled me into a side hug. "It looks great."

"No, that was definitely the Christmas elves that broke in." He laughed at my cheesiness. I could tell he was pleased by the look of the place, though. The hint of a smile he kept looking away to hide, remained despite his attempts to smother it.

He walked through the house into the kitchen to put down his keys and discovered more bags filled with decorations.

"We're not done yet are we?"

"Well," I pretended to ponder. "If you think this is too much, we can stop there."

He fished a pair of reindeer antler headbands I bought. "No, we definitely need to finish this."

"If you insist." I took one of the headbands from him and positioned it on my own head before yanking his shoulder down for him to crouch, so I could put one on his head as well. "Now we're ready to decorate."

Seeing him being dorky and willing to participate made my day. "Reese, you weren't using this ladder to hang up lights alone were you?" he asked accusingly. "I thought we agreed on waiting to do dangerous things for when I'm home."

"It's a ladder, not a tightrope."

He sighed heavily and gave me a look before following me to the porch with another bag of decorations. Together we put up a wreath, more lights (with Ryan on the ladder this time), and candy canes on both sides of our sidewalk leading to the front door.

"I'm going to make us some hot chocolate, it's freezing out there." I reached into our cabinet to pick out two mugs. "You can clock out for the night if you're tired, I know they've been pushing you in training."

"I'm fine," Ryan replied. He stood next to me while I got all the ingredients I wanted. Whoever said cooking together was a romantic or sexy idea was so wrong, there was nothing romantic about someone constantly being in the way.

I topped off our mugs with whipped cream and marshmallows before sitting down at the island with Ryan. He waited for me to sit before taking the seat next to me. Quiet music trailed into the room from the living room where I had a

Christmas playlist on. I couldn't quite tell which song was playing through the wall.

"Did you go to water aerobics today?"

I smirked a little into my mug. "Mhm, Sheryl's husband has pink eye, and you're not going to believe who *else* has pink eye."

"Sheryl?" he guessed. His ears were perked up, like they always did when I had town gossip for him. As much of an introvert as he was, he always loved when I had news for him from around town.

"Meredith!" Last month I told him about Sheryl telling everyone Meredith was a whore with no explanation or proof to back it up whatsoever. We both came up with theories as to why the two women had beef, and one of Ryan's hypotheses was that she came on to her husband.

He set down his mug. "No. Way."

I laughed at his quiet disbelief. "Yep, I asked Meredith's best friend why she wasn't in class this week, and it turns out she has none other than pink eye. Which is very contagious by the way."

Upon further contemplation, Ryan made a disgusted face. "I don't want to even imagine how they both managed to get it."

"Yeah, I was trying to ignore that part of it," I pointed out. "I didn't even know people had the energy for adultery at that age. You'd think they would settle with what they've got at age sixty."

"Once an adulterer, always an adulterer."

"Maybe they're in love or something," I offered.

He shot me a look over the rim of his mug. "No one falls in love whilst getting pink eye."

I propped my feet up on the footrest of his stool and turned

194

my body to face him. This was my favorite part of living together (officially) so far. The quiet moments. Sitting here at night just the two of us, made everything feel right. Everyone always tells you to marry your best friend, and there was no doubt about the fact Ryan had been my best friend for a very long time.

"Woah," I blurted out. My hand flew to my stomach out of instinct. "I think the baby is moving."

I looked up to Ryan to find him ready for anything and everything. He was tensed up like he was about to run into a burning building. Grabbing his hand, I pressed it to my stomach and waited for the weird fluttering feeling to happen again.

"I don't know if you'll feel it, but it feels like this," I grabbed his hand to press against it in a pulsing motion. "I'm probably too early for them to be kicking, but I think that's the baby moving."

He gently put both his hands back on my bump under my shirt and waited quietly. I watched him hunched over in his stool, bent so he could reach my stomach. We sat in silence for a few minutes before I put my hand in his hair to push it back.

"I don't feel it anymore, maybe it was just nothing."

His posture returned to its usual casual position, and I thought I saw a tear in his eye. "Let me know if you feel anything else," he said. He pulled out his phone, and I did my best to distract myself with my hot chocolate.

"I think it was the baby, Google says that's normal at this stage," he said out of nowhere. This whole time I thought he was checking work emails, but he was actually researching our baby. My rejection faded a little.

195

"Oh, hopefully they'll move around again so you can feel."

He nodded. "So, what's with the decorations all of a sudden? Is that for the baby too?"

"Yeah, I want to create traditions that we'll do every year. I figured this could be a practice run for us, so we can test what we like and what we don't."

"That's smart." He rubbed at his temple. "I like that little elf thing people do online."

I couldn't help but giggle at his admission. "We can definitely get an elf, are there any other things you'd want to do? I was thinking we could make pancakes for breakfast, or like fancy cinnamon rolls or something exciting."

"Are we doing the whole Christmas dinner with a turkey and everything too?" He looked much more stressed at that idea.

I shrugged. "That doesn't sound really exciting to me, is that something you want to do?"

"No, my mom tried that once and nearly burnt down the house."

"Okay, definitely no turkey." He noticed I was done with my hot chocolate and grabbed both our mugs to wash out in the sink. "Maybe we just make whatever sounds good that year, and we can switch up dinner. I think the most important part of the day for me is always the morning anyway."

"Yeah, the rest of the day should be dedicated to playing games and trying out your new presents," he agreed.

"And I think we can still do Santa, but maybe one present from him. The rest we can say are from us, so they don't brag to kids at school that Santa likes them better."

"We're already thinking about our kid going to school before they're out of the womb?"

"I'm already planning out their retirement celebration, Ryan. Catch up," I teased.

* * *

"Merry Christmas," I whispered, not wanting to scream at Ryan first thing after waking up, even though my heart was exploding at the sight of a fully decorated house on Christmas morning.

"Merry Christmas, Reese," he muttered. His hair was still a mess, and his pajamas were wrinkled like he wrestled a bear in his sleep. I patted the sofa cushion next to me for him to sit down on. He looked so cozy like this, I wished I could cuddle with him without it being weird, but I didn't want to give any mixed signals.

"Did you sleep well?" he asked.

I nodded quickly. "Yeah, I might have woken up super early though."

He glanced at the clock on his phone. "How long ago did you get up?"

"A couple hours ago," I said guiltily.

His eyebrows shot up. "You could've woken me up."

"I wanted you to get some rest, it's Christmas, no one should have to be woken up by an alarm clock."

"You are not an alarm clock, Reese."

"Whatever, you look like you slept well." He nodded. "Good, that's what matters."

He reached down to put my legs in his lap while he got a last few minutes of peace with his eyes closed. I did my best to wait patiently to start the day, it had been so many years since I experienced a real Christmas. As an adult, without any kids of my own or in my family, there wasn't really any big celebration other than going to my mom's for dinner. So this year was very exciting in my book.

"Should we make breakfast or open presents first?" he grumbled through his arm that was covering his face.

"Oh, I actually-" the oven beeping cut off my answer. "I guess it's done now."

Ryan moved his arm to quirk his brow at me. "I thought we were doing this together."

"We are, I just woke up earlier, so I thought I'd get it started."

"Alright then, let's go check it out." He gently set my legs back on the ground before getting up and leading us into the kitchen. "Maybe I could make bacon or something to go with your cinnamon rolls."

"I guess that would be fine," I said. "These need time to cool off anyway."

Ryan started pulling out pans and a pack of bacon from the fridge. Just the sight of it made me feel a little queasy, but I decided to stick it out. I moved the pan of homemade cinnamon rolls to the side and moved out of the way for Ryan to make his bacon.

We chatted mindlessly while the pan heated up, and the second that bacon hit the pan I tapped out. The raw meat sitting on the counter was already bad enough, but the smell of it cooking only emphasized the disgusting odor. I stood up and made the excuse that I needed to use the bathroom before sprinting out of the kitchen.

Once there, I splashed cold water on my cheeks. Minutes passed and my stomach still refused to settle, I couldn't get over how *bad* the bacon smelled. The last few months the smell of meat cooking wasn't my favorite, but usually it was bearable. This was a new level.

I sat down on the edge of the tub to rest my head in my hands. This was not how I wanted our first Christmas together to go. I rubbed my belly gently in hopes that soothing the baby would also soothe my sour stomach.

A soft knock sounded on the door. "Are you okay in there?"

"Yeah, all good." I called back. Shit. I must have been in here long enough for him to finish that damn bacon.

"You've been in here a while, what's going on?"

I stood up and opened the door. "Just a little nauseous is all," I winced at my weak voice.

"I'm sorry, why didn't you say anything?" He put his hand on my back to rub in circles gently. "Was it the bacon?"

"I didn't want to ruin the morning, it just smells awful to me."

He pushed up my chin, so I was looking him in the eyes. "You wouldn't have ruined anything, I'm sorry I didn't realize it would make you feel sick."

"I didn't either, it's usually not so bad, but sometimes when I cook meat it makes me feel sick now."

"Alright, we're a vegetarian household then." There was no hint of joking in his voice. "Would it be okay to go back in the kitchen or do I need to air out the house first?"

"I think I just need some water, and I'll be fine."

"I'll throw it away."

"Don't be silly, it's fine." I sat back on the stool slowly and gulped down the water Ryan handed me. "Yeah, I'm good now. You can go ahead and eat."

"You're not eating?"

The look on my face must have been enough to let him know I had no desire to eat anytime soon. He put the bacon in a to-go container and led me back to the living room. I continued nursing my ice water in hopes that I would magically want my cinnamon rolls again, but the thought of them made me even sicker.

"Let's just start with presents, we can eat later," he said.

The excitement of giving Ryan his gifts cheered me up. "Okay, here." I stood up to grab three presents around the tree that were for him. "These are yours."

"Reese," he reprimanded. "We said we were doing one small present for each other."

"These are three small things, no big deal." Truthfully, I had too many ideas for him. I couldn't pick just one gift, because I knew there were other things he would be happy to have. "Okay, go on, open up."

He made sure to shoot me a look before opening his presents. Two were video games he'd mentioned tons of times. I figured he wouldn't have much time to play games with the upcoming Olympics and a newborn baby around, but we still needed to make time for things we loved. He gave me a sweet hug before thanking me.

"One left," I pointed out. The last present was much smaller from the other two and a very familiar shape.

He shook the box and said, "I think I can guess what this is." I smiled at him and watched him open it. "Cards, I love them, thank you."

"They're not just cards, you have to open them."

I helped him open up the box to show him the custom cards, each with a unique hand painted design with volleyballs on them. My former student was a wonderful artist, and I commissioned her to make these a month ago for him. They came out even more beautiful than I could have imagined.

"Wow, how the hell did you get this done?"

"Beth." He looked at me a little confused. "My student, the one that works with Charlotte."

"Oh, wow, very cool." Carefully, he put the cards back in their box. "We'll have to play today."

I laughed at the sentiment. "I'm sure you'll be too busy playing your video games, but that's sweet."

"I'm never too busy to kick your ass in cards, Reese." He picked up a present wrapped in red plain red paper and handed it to me. "This one is yours."

I did my best to let go of any expectations. One of my worst traits was getting too excited for presents and getting all worked up only to be disappointed. Socks could be in this, or toothbrushes, and I needed to be okay with that. This day would not be ruined by my unrealistic expectations.

I gently slid my finger under the paper and pulled it open without ripping too much. I found a box with just an envelope inside. Had he just given me money? Honestly, I think that would have been the worst case scenario, that's what emotionally detached dads gave to their children. I gave a silent prayer that whatever was in this envelope was not money and opened it.

"No way," I said quietly. Looking up to him to make sure this was right, this wasn't a prank. My head went up and down looking from Ryan's face back down to the tickets in front of me. "You got me tickets to Broadway?"

His hand reached up to scratch at his neck nervously. "You'd enjoy that right? There's two tickets, and you don't have to take me. You can go with Georgia or someone else if you want."

"This is for Wicked," I emphasized. "Of course I'd enjoy that.

This is real?"

"Yeah, it's real."

"That's not small!" I argued. "I just got you video games and cards, and you got me *tickets to Broadway?*"

"It's Christmas, you go all out for this sort of thing, and I want you to be happy."

Screw not giving mixed signals, I practically jumped in his lap and wrapped my arms around his neck. Not only had he gone above and beyond, but it was personalized to me. He listened to me talking about Wicked and remembered it enough that when the time to get me a gift came around he decided this was a good idea.

It seemed small, but no one had given me such a thoughtful gift before. Every time a birthday or holiday came around, I was left with a slightly disappointed feeling because it felt like no one knew me enough to give me something personalized. But this was the *perfect* present.

I believed that loving people was knowing them, and Ryan definitely knew me. That was something I kept forgetting, and every time I did, he made a gesture like this to force me to remember. I squeezed the hell out of him before backing up and thanking him for the third time.

He brushed stray tears off my cheeks and gave me one last quick hug. "I'm glad you like it." His stomach growled obnoxiously loud. "Are you feeling hungry yet?"

I let out a wet laugh and agreed, "Yeah, let's go eat, and then we can open the presents for the baby."

After breakfast, we collectively opened the dozens of gifts we bought individually, along with presents from our friends and family. It was sort of like a mini baby shower. By the end of it all, we were surrounded by gender neutral baby clothes and toys. It made me even more excited for next year when we could celebrate with the baby here.

"Who knew present opening could be so exhausting?" I asked. "Our friends are so sweet, these are adorable." I held up a pair of tiny baby shoes Nick and Charlotte gifted us.

"It's crazy to think their feet will be so small." He picked up the little lion toy his mom gave us. "It'll be nice to put all this stuff in the baby's room when we've got their furniture."

I nodded. "Yeah, for now we can keep it all together until we have the room figured out." Bracing on the couch behind me, I pushed myself up onto it. "Ready for your video games?"

"No, we can do something else together."

I scoffed. "You obviously want to play, and I'm kind of curious about this Elden Ring one, can we play together?"

His head whipped around to me. "You want to play?"

"Yeah, some of my kids told me about it, it seems interesting."

And that was how we spent the rest of Christmas, playing Elden Ring. I had to admit the game was pretty addicting, and seeing him nerd out about runes and our skill tree was endearing. For the most part, he let me control the game to run around and adventure, but when it came to fighting, I handed it back to him.

While it wasn't how I planned the day to go, it was more fun than anything I could have decided for us ahead of time.

Chapter 22

Reese

School was back to normal, and Ryan's training camp was approaching closer day by day. As his friend, I was excited for him to be one step closer to such a major moment in his career. However, as the pregnant mother of his child, I was apprehensive about being left to my own devices.

It was weird to think about, a few months ago I spent all of my time at home alone. Granted, I wasn't home much because I found ways to keep myself busy, but I was independent. Ryan made things much easier, all of the chores I never wanted to do, he naturally picked up doing over time.

Knowing he was there to bounce ideas off of, and talk through insecurities about becoming parents helped a lot. I was scared to lose that. The idea of finding out I had grown too used to him and become less independent, or even reliant on him was terrifying.

Walking through our front door, I found him on the couch reading our current parenting improvement book. So far we had gotten through four of them, and they did a lot to ease our worries about not knowing enough. The books answered questions I hadn't even thought to ask.

"Hey," he greeted. "The rest of the nursery furniture arrived a couple of hours ago."

"Great, we should get started on that since you'll be leaving soon."

He looked at his fake watch. "Where am I going?"

"Training camp," I deadpanned.

He set the book down on our side table and stood up with a questioning look on his face. "That's not for a few more weeks, and I won't be gone forever."

"I know, it's just a thought." I set down my bags and filled up my water cup again. No matter how much water I drank lately, I still felt dehydrated.

"Anything happen at work?" he said cautiously. "Your mean old principal give you any trouble?"

"No, she's pretty much avoided me like the plague since your Thanksgiving stunt." Not that I was complaining, between studying for the baby, constantly feeling tired, and teaching my classes I had no time for her nonsense.

"Well that's good right?"

"If I don't ever want a promotion, I guess."

He rubbed my back soothingly. "Why don't I make us some dinner and you can watch one of your Netflix shows."

I sighed out of frustration. "I have work to grade, and we need to set up the nursery. There isn't time to just lay around and do nothing."

"Okay, what if you grade and when I'm done I can-"

"How am I going to do this when you aren't here?" Pure emotion flooded into my voice. Everything I was feeling punched into every word like a cross stitch craft.

He stood frozen for a moment before gently guiding me to

205

sit on a stool next to him. "I'll just be gone for a few weeks, and then-"

"No, I mean all the other times you'll have to leave. When the baby is here and I have to somehow juggle being a mom and a teacher and a friend, and a person with interests and hobbies and-"

"We'll figure out how to balance it out, it won't all be on you."

"But it will, because you'll be gone, and I will be the only one here. Unless you're proposing I get up and leave to the other side of the world every other month or so."

"Are you regretting your decision?"

That broke my heart a little. "No, I just don't know how to do this." My hands moved between us frantically. "I can't just turn it on and off, one day I'm a co-parent and the next I'm a single mom doing everything on my own."

"I can still just back out and get a normal job, I haven't signed any contracts yet in terms of playing. I could just do the training camp and be done with it."

"No." I hung my head in my hands. "No, that is the last thing that I want."

I took a breath to gather my thoughts, he was trying to fix my problem. The issue with that was that there was no fix. No solution to my fear other than to try it out and take things day by day.

"I am just terrified of becoming my mother," I confessed. "I still want to be me, Reese, the person, not a woman whose sole personality is being a mother and resenting her child for it."

He nodded solemnly, and I thought he sort of understood, as much as a man possibly could. "My worst fear is being an absent father," he said quietly. "I think our fear proves that we are the opposite of our parents. Your mother never worried so much about being a good mom, she was so focused on herself. And my dad certainly never cared."

I let out another breath and grabbed his hand closest to me. "I want you to go through with this Olympics training because that's who you are. Your first love was volleyball, that is your whole life. And to be a good parent means you need to be happy."

"I would be happy, here with you." I didn't believe him for a second. "Truly, I would."

"We can do this, with you being away on occasion, I'm just scared. That's all." He wrapped his arms around me in a hug and I let him comfort me. "We should really go set up the nursery though, the boxes are taking up like half of our garage."

He laughed into my hair and pulled away. "Would it make you feel better to get it taken care of now?"

"Definitely," I confirmed. "And maybe we could order takeout? No offense, but you suck at cooking."

He gave me a disapproving look while pulling out his phone. "Rude," he chided. "Indian or pizza?"

* * *

I took another bite of cheesy goodness and winced a little at the burnt roof of my mouth. Currently, Ryan sat in front of me putting together a tiny bookshelf while my job was reading the instructions out for him. Pictures. All of the instructions were pictures.

"I can help after this slice," I insisted.

"I've got it, it's probably more difficult to do with two people." He swore as he slammed his finger between two pieces of wood.

"I can just start on another box then." He looked up from his project to glare at me. "You can't expect me to just sit here and watch you the whole time."

"You're helping with the instructions."

I sassily held up the booklet filled with pictures. "How is this helping? You haven't looked at it once."

"Because I have you looking at it for me."

"So we're doing Ikea furniture instruction telepathy?"

He hummed and continued working. I rolled my eyes and leaned back against the pillow Ryan brought for me to sit on. Even our rocking chair still needed to be put together, the furniture industry had successfully made us pay to put together all of our stuff.

Once I polished off my slice of pizza, I stood up to grab the box I was most excited for, the bassinet. "I'll do that next. Why don't you start putting their clothes in the dresser or something?"

"Are you seriously not going to let me build anything?"

"Some of this stuff is heavy, and," he paused to force a screw into a pre-drilled hole. "It's annoying as hell."

"Maybe it would be less annoying if you looked at the instructions," I suggested helpfully.

He laughed and put down his tools for a second to take a break. "Alright, have at it Macgyver."

I picked up the booklet and examined his work. He spilled the different kinds of screws together on the floor, so it took a minute, but eventually I realized he had one of the wooden sides upside down and used the wrong screws on the wrong holes.

"Oh, seems like they should have made that clearer," he

murmured.

I smiled at his stubbornness and grabbed the bassinet box to start on it again. As I reached for the box cutter, Ryan stopped me again. "I can take care of this part."

"You do realize I use these at school all the time right?"

He clicked his tongue at me. "That place is the worst." Suddenly, he sat upright. I watched him mull over his words before speaking again. "Would you be happier at another job?"

"What do you mean?"

"If you could do anything, what would you do?"

"So on top of moving houses, having a baby, and sharing a living space with someone else for the first time, you want me to add a career change to life changing events this year?"

"Just humor me."

I took a few minutes to really think about his question while I started twisting together plastic pieces. In theory there were a lot of jobs I would love to do, but in reality, I was sure I would miss teaching. I would hate to be alone all day, so I needed to be around people. Adult people were draining, so kids or teenagers were preferable. And I couldn't think of any profession other than teaching that fit that criteria.

"I think I would still want to be a teacher." I could tell he didn't believe me whatsoever from his slight frown. "I would definitely change the school and the circumstances, like my principal, and all the government standards we're held to. But I like being a teacher."

"Are there any other schools that you think would be better nearby? You could try the elementary school to get away from that horrible lady."

His dedication to hating my principal when he didn't even know her name was admirable. "I just don't think it would be worth it, I still would have to follow standards and have ridiculously long hours."

"Okay, well, something to keep in mind if this lady gets worse. I hate seeing you come home all stressed out."

"I'm not stressed out," I argued.

He paused for a moment. "Are you serious?"

"Yeah, I love my job."

"Baby, you come home every day pissed off at the world. You nearly cut my head off earlier for offering to cook while you graded."

Did I? I was a little testy earlier, but I felt perfectly normal after eating. "I think that's just baby hormones, I feel fine now."

He seemed skeptical to continue pushing the subject, but spoke anyway, "I remember you doing this before you were pregnant. You take a few hours to decompress after work and you're fine, but for the first hour or so when you get home you seem miserable."

"Oh," I said dumbly. "I didn't realize I was like that."

"It's not a bad thing, I mean it *is*. I don't mind hearing you rant, though. You never do it in public, only when it's the two of us at home. I just want to make sure you're happy, because you don't seem like it."

"I'll try to be more conscious of it then."

"No," he slapped his face. "I want you to tell me the honest truth, if you're truly happy at work and are just venting it's fine. It's just sometimes you say things that make me think you're unhappy there, and if that's the case we should fix it."

He set the fully finished bookshelf to the side and grabbed a new box. "I'll think about it," I said, genuinely meaning it. The last few years at work had been a rollercoaster. I had, and would, always love teaching, but the downsides were hard to ignore. Especially with a baby on the way.

Chapter 23

Ryan

Usually, I was filled with relief at the thought of volleyball season coming up soon. Now, I felt only dread. Reese and I were working on communicating how we felt, which was much harder than it sounded. Especially for her. Sometimes, she held in her feelings for so long they just bursted out of her unexpectedly.

The decision to go through with playing in the Olympics was still weighing heavily on my mind. I still had time to back out. Reese would lose her mind, she kept insisting on this being the only choice, but I didn't want to miss out on precious memories with her and our baby. She was also downplaying her worries about me being gone. Only in the moments that her emotions built up was she completely honest about how scared she was.

I did my best to comfort her when she was open about it. I even offered to get a job at Nick's diner as a busboy, and boy did she hate that idea. We were still in a gray area in our relationship, officially we were friends, but it felt like more.

Asking her for a real relationship when I was putting all of

212

this strain on her felt selfish. And that was the opposite of what I wanted to be. In fact, I vowed to not be selfish when it came to Reese and our child. I would do anything for them, even if the hardest thing was keeping some distance when it came to Reese.

The bell over the door chimed as I walked into Reid's Diner. I looked to the countertop to find the two people I needed to speak to, conveniently in one place. Joining them, I slid onto a barstool and reached over to steal a menu from Ashton.

"Hey, didn't expect to see you here," he said. "Thought you'd be on your way to New York by now."

"I'm leaving in the morning." I nodded to Nick as he walked up to us. "I need a favor."

"Yeah, anything," Nick replied, his hands busy carrying plates to Ashton.

"I need you both to keep an eye out for Reese while I'm gone. She's never going to ask for help, and if anything will offer to help you with shit." I lowered my voice to ensure they were listening, "but I need you to not ask anything of her while I'm gone. No dog sitting, or babysitting, or helping with random side projects you decide to do. Don't ask her."

The twins both shared a look and turned to me. "Yeah, of course, man."

"It's important, she has a lot going on already. I know she's everyone's go-to for help, but now isn't the time. And if you have time, I would appreciate you helping her, however you want."

"Is she doing okay?"

"Yeah, she's great. She's just anxious about the baby coming, and me leaving definitely is not helping." I stole a fry off of Ashton's plate. "I just want to make sure she's okay while I'm

213

gone."

"That's awfully friendly of you."

I rolled my eyes. "Yeah, well, she is the mother of my child."

"But you're just friends."

I stood up to make my exit. "That's up to her. But I'm working on it, just give me some time."

Their smiles grew, and they both patted whatever part of me they could reach. "Finally, it took you half your life."

"Imagine how I feel," I muttered under my breath. That only encouraged their goofy hoots and hollers. "Anyways, I have more stops to make on my goodbye tour. See you in a month or so."

"We'll look out for her while you're gone, man. Have a safe trip."

Thankfully, my next stop was right next door. I walked into Brewing Pages, the local bookstore and coffee shop that Charlotte owned. She had a few customers huddled around the countertop, so I decided to peruse the small parenting book section while I waited.

"Hey," Charlotte greeted from behind me. I put the book I was holding down and turned around to greet her. "You can have that if you want."

"I'll buy it," I said. Following her over to the register, I tried to remember my rehearsed lines. I didn't know Charlotte as well as I knew the rest of our group. We went to school together, but she was a few grades above me, and neither of us were super chatty.

She put the book in a brown paper bag for me and pushed it across the counter. "Coffee?"

"No, I'm okay." I held the bag awkwardly and looked over at the colorful menu board next to us. "I just wanted to ask if you could check in on Reese while I'm away. I don't know if she told you already, but I'll be gone for about a month. If you could make sure she takes some time to have fun and relax, that would be great."

"Yeah, I can do that." She crossed her arms over her chest. "It's nice of you to ask."

"She has a habit of helping everyone but herself, as I'm sure you've noticed. I'll still be there for her too, of course, but it's harder to do over the phone."

"I get it. She does a lot for me, I'm happy to return the favor."

"Great, well I should get going." I paused when I remembered I hadn't paid yet. "How much do I owe you?"

"Nothing, consider it an early baby shower gift."

"Thanks again, Charlotte."

"No problem." She waved to me as I turned to walk out the door.

* * *

I knocked on the door to Ashton and Georgia's house quietly. Out of fear of waking their newborn baby, I decided the bell was not a great option. Reese said she was expecting me, so the quiet knock should suffice.

"Hey, Ryan," she greeted. The door opened to reveal Ruth, Ashton's first daughter, standing behind Georgia at the door.

"Hey, Reese asked me to drop this off for you guys for Ruth's bake sale." It was a dozen white chocolate macadamia cookies. "I also need to ask you something if that's okay."

"Yeah," she backed up to wave me inside. "Come in, the baby's awake so you can say hi if you want."

"Great," I breathed out. As we walked through to the living

room I scanned all the pictures hung up of the four of them. Through the arched walkway, I also saw artwork on the fridge that I could only assume was Ruth's. This was a home. I needed to get more pictures of myself and Reese when I could.

In the living room, the baby was laid on her stomach on a blanket. "We're working on her neck muscles," Georgia joked. I read about tummy time in my books, so it wasn't a shocking sight.

"She's growing so fast."

"Yeah, I blink and a whole day goes by. It really is amazing how every week she makes so much progress."

I tried not to think about the fact that those were milestones I could miss out on with my baby. Just a week of time away was enough to be behind. "I wanted to talk to you about Reese."

"Okay, is it a serious conversation?" She turned to Ruth, who was already absorbed in her coloring book.

"No, she can stay. I just need a favor," I said.

"Alright, what can I do?"

"I'm not sure if Reese mentioned it, but I'm going to be gone for about a month starting tomorrow." She nodded. "If you could check in on her when you get a chance, that would be great."

I let out a breath and leaned back on the couch cushions. "You clearly already have a lot going on, but I just wanted to let you know she's a little stressed with the baby coming and me leaving. She could use a friend to rely on. Even if it's something small like giving her advice on how to keep our houseplants alive."

"Of course, I can definitely do that. Honestly, I've been so disconnected from everything since having Harper. Ashton and I hardly leave the house, so it would be good to spend time with a friend again."

"Good, well again, no pressure since I know you've got a lot going on. Just a phone call checking in on her is enough."

"She'll be just fine," Georgia assured. The baby next to us started fussing, and Georgia leaned over to pick her up. "I'm glad she has you looking out for her."

I nodded and stood, taking my cue to leave. "I'll see myself out since your hands are full. Enjoy your cookies, Ruth. Thanks again, Georgia."

"Thanks for stopping by."

* * *

Will's office never failed to amaze me. Completely different from the rest of Rosewood, his corporate highrise made me feel like I teleported to a major city in Europe every time. I waited for his secretary to notify him of my presence and did my best to not look uncomfortable.

He stepped out in a suit, and I nearly laughed. Unlike the rest of us, Will kept his job separate from his personal life. I still had no clue what he did all day other than sit in a nice office and have people fetch him coffees, not that it mattered.

"Hey, come in."

"Not sure I'm dressed for the occasion, but okay." I sat in the chair opposite his desk. "I'm kind of in a rush, sorry to interrupt your day, but I need a favor."

"What is it?"

"I'm leaving tomorrow for training camp, and I need you to look out for Reese." In practice, he was the best out of the men we knew to comfort her when she was upset. "She's already stressed, and I'm not doing anything to help that. So I need

217

you to check up on her if you can."

"So just stop by the house?" He didn't look enthused at the idea.

"Well she's not really there much, she works long hours."

"Does she do anything else regularly?"

"Water aerobics?"

He snorted. "Water aerobics."

"Yeah, if you wanted to run into her at the gym on Thursday nights and make sure she gets home okay, that would be great."

"You want me to stalk your girlfriend-"

"Friend, haven't earned that title yet."

"Your friend that you got pregnant, after her water aerobics class," he clarified.

"You don't have to stalk her, you can say hello. She doesn't bite."

He sighed and moved around pens on his desk. "I can do that."

"Good, thanks man. If she mentions doing anything dangerous that requires a ladder, maybe offer to help her."

"Got it."

"Great, I really appreciate it. I owe you."

* * *

That night, I got home after dark to find Reese dozing off on the couch. I deflated a little since I planned on spending time with her before I left for training. School had kept her busy lately though, so I understood her exhaustion.

I leaned down to pick her up from the couch and carry her up to her bedroom. She stirred a little as my arms scooped under her, but otherwise stayed asleep. Her room was still

218

mostly empty despite us having lived here for a couple of months. So was mine, I intentionally left space in case we ever wanted to share it.

Pulling back the covers, I placed her down and wrapped the blankets around her. Reese was always a deep sleeper. The amount of times that I'd carried her to bed in the last few months were ridiculous. I sat on the edge of the bed next to her for a minute while I rested my hand on her stomach.

"Hey, this is your dad speaking," I whispered into the quiet night air. "You might have heard that I'm leaving for a few weeks. I just wanted to tell you I'll be home soon, try to go easy on your mom while I'm gone."

I stood to go scavenge some dinner before bed. Then halted when I remembered there was something else I wanted to say. I kneeled next to the bed and spoke to the baby in her belly.

"And I always will. Be home soon, I mean. Anytime you or your mom need anything, I'll be there." I sighed and cringed at how awkward it was talking to myself. "Just wanted you to know."

I stood up again to leave when I heard Reese's gravely voice pipe up, "Do you mean that?"

I winced. "Sorry, I thought you were asleep."

"You were practicing." She gave me a small smile over the blanket tucked under her chin.

"I was." We stayed silent for a beat. "Have you eaten yet?"

"Yeah, but I can go sit with you while you eat. There are leftovers in the fridge."

"You can sleep if you're tired, Reese. I know you've had a long day."

She sat up in bed and reached for my hand to help her up. I did, and when she was on her feet, she wrapped me up in a hug. I let out a breath and leaned into her, resting my chin on her head while she warmed me up.

"I know it's selfish, but I'm not ready for you to go," she admitted.

My heart shattered into about a million pieces. "I can still stay." Contractually, I couldn't. But if she asked me to, I would, and I'd spend all day tomorrow figuring out a new job.

"No, you can't." She pulled back from the hug and gave me a sad smile. "Come on, you must be starving, it's late."

"Will you be okay while I'm gone? I'll still call every morning and night, there just isn't time to travel back and forth since the days are like eighteen hours."

"Yes, for the hundredth time, I'll be fine."

We quietly walked downstairs together to the kitchen. I rummaged through the fridge while she sat at the island opposite me. "If you do need anything while I'm gone, tell me and I'll get it done or have someone help you."

"Okay," she agreed. I knew she wouldn't dare actually do that though. She was Reese, and that meant she took care of everything herself. "I'm mostly sad that you'll miss out on finding the gender."

I winced. "I can probably be on the phone if you give me a heads up that day."

"Yeah, that would be good." Her expression didn't match her words.

I wasn't sure if it was more painful to acknowledge our shitty situation since there was no perfect fix or to just ignore it completely. We could tell ourselves everything was fine all we wanted, but neither of us would really know what it was like until we were actually in it. All I could do was prepare the best I could to set her up to be happy.

Chapter 24

Reese

Living alone felt different. I blamed it on how big the house was, every night I came home to empty rooms and dead silence. Nothing soothed the lonely feeling. Except for Ryan's calls, it was a good distraction to hear updates from him.

It was almost like when he was playing in Europe and would call every now and then to check in. The thought that not much had changed since then bothered me. He was still off living his life, and here I was. Stuck at home having his baby. My entire world was changed, yet he was just continuing on the same as always.

To avoid lingering on that thought for too long, I kept myself as busy as possible. Which wasn't hard, I had plenty of work to keep me busy. I was a regular at Charlotte's coffee shop until close so I didn't have to sit alone in this damn house for so long.

Our friends were around much more than usual. I wasn't sure if that was because I was looking for things to do, or they were all worried about me. It wasn't exactly fun being pregnant and alone.

My principal was also getting more and more relentless with asking me to help her prepare ideas and presentations for her bosses. The only way I could think to avoid that was leaving school as soon as the bells rang. Ryan was right, if I started doing things for her again she wouldn't stop asking. And I didn't have time to stay at school for twelve hours a day with a newborn baby.

Which led me to my next recurring worry. How would I do this with a baby? Even leaving on time, I hated the idea of abandoning my baby to be with complete strangers. They weren't even born yet, and I couldn't stop myself from reading and watching every horror story about daycares that I came across.

My phone ringing stopped my spiral. "Hey."

"How was your day?" Ryan sounded half asleep, and his voice made me sink deeper into my bed to get comfortable.

"Good, yeah."

"Good, I'm glad." There was a pause. "Any other updates on the kids who were fighting yesterday?"

"They're suspended, other than that it's been pretty quiet," I answered. Another long silence. "How was your day?"

"Fine, a lot of cardio. I was running around the city earlier and saw a painting that reminded me of you. I bought it since you said we needed more wall decorations.

"Oh, that's sweet, thanks." I tried to think of more words to keep the conversation going, but my mind drew a blank.

"Reese, are you okay?"

"Yeah, you already asked that. I'm just a little tired."

"Maybe we should try calling in the middle of the day. I feel like I get you right when you're busy in the morning and when you're getting ready for bed at night."

"That could be good," I replied while rubbing my eyes.

"Or maybe I should try writing letters again, you don't seem very chatty."

"What do you mean *again?*" At this point, I had no clue what we were even talking about. I was just happy to listen to his voice.

"Like when I was in Germany. The letters I wrote you," he spoke like I was purposefully being dense.

"What letters?"

A long pause. When he spoke, the words came out a little too fast, "Never mind, have you felt anything more from the baby?"

"Yeah, still the same little flutters. I don't think they're quite kicks yet, but it feels like they're getting there."

I fell asleep at some point because when I woke up my phone was still pressed against my cheek, leaving a rectangle impression on my face when I went to wash my face the next morning. I really needed to go to bed earlier, or take a nap in the middle of the day like an old person.

* * *

Every day went by frustratingly slowly. Each one more painful than the last. Especially with it getting dark so early in the day, I felt like I was banished from ever seeing the sun again. My friends were the only saving grace, especially Charlotte.

I helped her with wedding planning in between finishing grading. Though my mood must have been obvious, because she stopped me as soon as I walked in. She asked if we could have dinner together instead of just sitting in the lobby of her coffee shop, so I obliged.

"This is amazing," I said with another roll already in my hand.

Charlotte sat on the couch next to me and handed me a napkin. "Right? Benefits of marrying a chef, he also knows all the greatest restaurants in a fifty mile radius."

"Yeah, you're lucky."

I continued stuffing my face to avoid having to answer any potential questions. Usually, I was much better at hiding bad days. However, every day for the past couple of weeks had been bad, and I was starting to forget what a good day looked like. The worst part was that I didn't even know what was wrong. I was just in a sour mood.

"How is school?"

"Good."

"And the baby? You mentioned you had an appointment last week."

"Also good."

"Reese," she pushed the basket of rolls away from me slightly. "What's going on? You aren't like yourself."

This was one of my recurring nightmares. Something about people asking if I was okay when I was on the verge of a breakdown always made me snap. I didn't want her to see me cry, and I definitely didn't want to make her feel like she had to fix my problems.

The tears streamed down my face before I even opened my mouth. "Oh, Reese."

She moved closer to me on the couch and wrapped her arms around me. "I'm sorry, I don't really know what's wrong. I'm just so sad all the time."

"Yeah," she sat up to rub my back. "I've noticed. Is there anything I can do to help?"

"No." I looked around at her old apartment and dread filled my stomach. "I just hate going home to that empty house. It's so depressing."

"Oh. Do you want to stay here?"

"What? No. I can't just commandeer your apartment for no reason."

"No one's staying here, the bed is comfy. And Nick and I are right next door if you need anything."

"That would be silly, I'm a grown woman and I have a house-"

"Reese, please stay." She looked directly into my eyes. "Really, I'm worried about you. It would make me feel much better if you stayed."

"You really don't mind?"

"Not one bit." She took another bite of bread. "When we're done eating we'll go to your place and get anything you need."

* * *

Charlotte's second floor apartment resided over her bookstore. It was a studio, and while she moved in with Nick months ago, the place still felt lived in. Her record player sat dusty in the corner, so I took the luxury of cleaning it up and picking out a vinyl from her collection.

I fell asleep in minutes. It was an amazing feeling compared to the hours I stayed up, staring at my ceiling the night before. I didn't even set an alarm, since it was the weekend, and I had sleep to catch up on, I figured it would be better to go without.

When I woke up, I grabbed the bag of my things Charlotte drove me home to get the night before. This would be my temporary home for now, at least until Ryan got back. I couldn't keep staying in that house alone. It was supposed to be a happy place, somewhere to feel safe.

It was too ironic that I imagined moving my mom into that house as a kid to help her get back out into the world. Yet I felt trapped in it.

Chapter 25

Ryan

It was safe to say I didn't make any friends at training camp. A few of them I had even met or knew from previous run-ins, but I had no energy to be extroverted. My thoughts only consisted of performing well enough to get onto the team, and Reese.

Every call it sounded like she had less words to offer me. I had no idea what to say either, terrified of crossing the line of more than friends, only to have her run away from me. One step forward, two steps back. When I left, I was hopeful that this time apart would be less stressful than we expected. I was so fucking wrong.

Her voice was proof enough that things weren't going well back home. The back and forth of hoping we would get together as a couple was messing with my head, too. I wondered if she was regretting having anything to do with me in the first place.

Maybe she would ask Clay for help. He had a stable job, somewhat reasonable hours. Always in town, always around even when on the clock to help her out. She felt comfortable enough to ask him to help us move. I could only remember one time she ever trusted me to help her with something, and that required damn near begging.

Here I was, a complete moron, hours away from my pregnant best friend while she was struggling to come to terms with being a parent. At least we had one thing in common. I promised to be better for her, for both of them, and I was failing.

I eventually fell asleep to the torturous thoughts of Reese deserving better than I was able to give. Dreams and nightmares usually escape me. Even if I had them, I almost never remembered them. But this time was different.

In a cold sweat, I woke up with a start. I swung my legs to the side only to kick the nightstand next to me by accident and stood with a few curses thrown into the air. Reese needed me, and I wasn't there for her.

The training camp still had a few days left. From other training and recruiting trips I'd experienced before, not much happened in the last few days other than networking anyway. I pulled my laptop out of my bag and sat on a plush striped armchair in the corner of my hotel room.

I made sure to copy in all trainers and managers that I'd met in my time here, including my own manager. The email was quick and to the point. I didn't even bother to spell check or re-read, the gist was what mattered. That was made clear by the opening line, 'Call me if you want me to play for your team. I'm going home to the love of my life, who is pregnant and needs me.'

And home I went.

Not without a few pit stops first. I knocked on the door to Reese's mother's house and waited a significant amount of time, only to see her mom looking at me through the window behind a curtain.

"It's just me, Ms. Finch. I need to pick up something for Reese, could you let me in please?"

I waited impatiently for her to open the door a crack. "What do you want?"

"Can I come in? I was wondering about some mail I sent her a while back. I think it might still be here."

She opened the door a smidge more, and I took that as my in. I sidestepped past her and into the house. "I don't know what you're talking about, boy."

"Mail. If mail comes for Reese, what do you do with it?"

"Not much does." She stared at me through her thin glasses. "I guess I would probably put it in the attic. She never remembers to pick up stuff when I tell her."

I made my way through the small house without much room to walk. It certainly wasn't made for a man my size, I had to tuck in my elbows to avoid knocking over lamps and trinkets. She showed me the pull down door in the ceiling, and I pulled it down slowly.

I turned around to look at her feeble stature. "Ms. Finch, how do you even get up here?"

"I'm old, but not that old. And if it's light I usually just toss it up."

That was a distressing thought. I let out a breath and prepared myself for whatever it was I was about to find up there. There could be anything, and there could be a lot of it. I just hoped my letters were somewhere in the mix.

Piles and piles of boxes and loose papers greeted me. I pulled myself up to sit on the ledge and turned on my phone flashlight. That was a grim sight. It could take days to go through all of this, and I really didn't have that kind of time.

A couple of hours of sorting and Reese's mom called up to me, "I told you, you're not going to find it. She doesn't get much mail here."

"This is important, Ms. Finch. I'll just keep looking if you don't mind."

Her huff and a grumble under her breath, that I suspected was her saying she *did* mind, only encouraged me to move faster. I was going to find those damn letters if it was the last thing I did. This whole time I thought Reese didn't care or was too busy to respond to them. I was hoping if she read them, she might see how I saw her. And would understand why I would never let her down.

In my search, I came across a college ruled piece of paper with both mine and Reese's handwriting. Our marriage contract. I wasn't sure of the legitimacy considering we signed it with pencil on the same sheet of her math homework, but it was worth keeping. I tucked it in my back pocket and continued searching.

"Now that I think of it, there's a patterned plaid box up there that might have what you're looking for."

"Sorry, Ms. Finch. Say that again?"

"The plaid box. Look in there."

I moved around the stacks of paper that I already had organized to look at the wall of boxes behind it. On the far bottom right I found one that looked plaid. Sitting on top of a few of the bigger boxes, I set down my flashlight to give off enough light for me to see as I opened it up.

Immediately, I recognized my own messy writing staring back at me. I flipped through the letters to see if any were opened, and while most were sealed shut, a few of the older letters were messily ripped at the top. The letters were all still housed inside, thankfully.

"Yeah, found it, coming down now."

I climbed back down the ladder and pushed the stairs to the attic back up into the ceiling for her. We shared a look before I begrudgingly asked, "So Reese never got these?"

"I can't remember dear, it was years ago. Probably not if they're still here."

"Some of these are open, was that you?"

She crossed her arms angrily and took a big step back. "Are you accusing me of something in my own home?"

"No ma'am, this was all I needed. I'll be going home now."

* * *

I got home to an empty house. By the looks of it, Reese hadn't been here all night despite it being a Saturday morning. My hands shook while I pulled out my phone and pressed the call button next to her contact.

"Good morning," her sleepy voice answered. Instant relief flooded through my body.

"Where are you?" I couldn't hide the worry in my voice.

Muffled sounds filled my ear and I almost asked her again. "I'm just getting ready."

"Okay, but where?"

"Oh, I forgot to tell you," she said guiltily. I recognized the white lie from the one her mother told me earlier. "I'm staying at Charlotte's old apartment for a few days."

"What?"

"Yeah, I think I just needed a change of scenery."

"Right. We just moved into this house a couple of months

231

ago, Reese."

"Are you here? In Rosewood?" The sleepiness in her voice had disappeared.

"Just hold tight. We'll talk in a little bit." I grabbed the box and my keys and ran back out to my car.

I did my best to knock quietly on the backdoor of Charlotte's shop. The annoyed look on her face when she swung the door open told me I failed. "Hey, I need to talk to Reese. Can I come in?"

She hesitated before letting me in. "I thought you weren't supposed to be back until next week."

"I'm a little early."

"Okay, well she's upstairs. Try not to scare her, she spooks easily."

I nodded and headed through the corridor to take the stairs two at a time. "Thanks," I called.

I knocked again, more quietly this time, and waited. A shy looking Reese greeted me and pulled the door open enough for me to walk in. The second floor apartment felt spacious since there were no walls separating the living areas. I stepped inside and turned around to see how she was handling my sudden appearance.

"Did something happen? Why did you leave training camp early?" Her pajamas were rumpled, and the sight of her messy hair made my tension ease.

"No, I just wanted to see you. The important part of it was over anyway."

"What? I thought you said you can't leave early?"

"You're technically not supposed to, but you needed me here," I confessed.

She sat on the couch and patted the seat beside her. "I was

doing okay, it's just been... difficult adjusting to being alone again."

"I think it's important that we're honest with each other." I grabbed her hands gently and pulled them into my lap. "It was hard for me too."

Her eyes strayed down to our joined hands. "I just sort of feel like you're moving on without me, you're still continuing on with your life while mine is on complete pause."

I nodded. "I never want you to feel that way. *You* are my life. We're creating a family together, and that is my whole world. I don't think you're hearing me when I say I'm still willing to get a normal job and stay here with you."

"Because I don't want you to," she insisted. "Even if you didn't resent me, I would never forgive myself."

"And I would never forgive myself if I ruined this because of a stupid job."

"It's your dream."

I sighed and placed the box tucked under my arm on the coffee table in front of us. "This is my dream. It's all written in here, maybe not explicitly because I was too chicken shit to say it, but you should read these."

Reese sat up to rifle through the dozens of letters I'd written to her in my time overseas. "I mailed them to you," I clarified. "I sent them to your mom's address since I wasn't sure about your apartment's address, thinking she would give it to you. But she never did."

She was silent as she picked up one of the open envelopes and slipped a handwritten letter out of it. It took approximately sixty seconds for her to start crying. I leaned back into the sofa and waited for her to finish. When she was done with that letter she set it to the side and continued to the next without even looking at me.

Pages of neatly stacked letters filled the table by the time she was done. Stunned, she stared at the wall before turning to me. "You wrote all of this, for me."

"Yes."

"I never knew."

"Nope, clearly not." I put my hands behind my head. "I thought you were too busy, or only interested in Clay. You started dating him about halfway through these. So I let it go."

"How could you think that?" she cried. "These are," she picked up pages and flipped through them to skim through lines. "Beautiful. They're beautiful."

"It was a while ago, so I don't remember exactly what I said. Just that it was pretty painfully obvious how I felt." I picked up one of the pages she was holding to read the first line. "Do you understand now? Even when I was away, I was still just thinking about you."

"I had no idea." She turned to face her body toward me. "Your phone calls were so short, I figured you were just checking in out of obligation."

"No, I was trying to remain *friendly*. Since it was obvious that's what you wanted."

"That isn't what I want. If I've learned anything over these past couple of weeks, it's that I want you around even more. I thought being friends and raising a baby together would be okay, but it's not. It feels like I'm ripping my heart in two trying to figure out how to act, what to think, what to *feel*."

"I love you." Her eyes widened. "In all of our efforts to be there for each other, we somehow managed to push each other apart too."

She smiled at me. "I love you, too."

I wrapped her up in a hug and listened to her little sniffles. I missed her hugs, the smell of her shampoo, the feeling of her pressed against me. Even though we were halfway across town, I suddenly felt like I was home. Reese was my home.

"So, we're getting married then, yeah?" she joked.

"Reese, don't steal my thunder please." She frantically looked around for any indications of a jewelry box. "I'm joking, baby, unless you want to get married now. I figured we would go at our own pace, since we've already done things a little out of order."

"We have the rest of our lives," she said dreamily. "To be clear, I still want you to try out for the Olympics if that's still on the table."

"Honey-"

"Listen, I did have an epiphany while I've been staying here. I do love teaching, but I think I might want to start teaching a different demographic. What if I worked at a daycare while our baby goes there?"

She took in a gulp of air to continue her explanation. "It's the best of both worlds, I still get to have a job and do what I love, and I don't have to leave our baby for hours and hours every day. There's a pretty nice one just a half hour from us. And there would be no more dealing with crazy principals, or grading. I doubt six month olds have much homework."

"I like this idea. And it would make you happy?"

"Yeah, I think so. It works for our schedule much better, and you still get to live out the peak of your athletic career."

"I don't want you to feel like your life is on pause."

"This would fix that, my career workload will be much less. Plus, if we're really giving this a go, being lovers and parents, it takes a weight off my shoulders."

"Lovers, I like that title." She chuckled at my stupid joke.

"I was kind of freaking out about how this would go long term, the thought of you bringing home a girlfriend made me cry at least three nights in a row. The world is spinning again."

I sighed and lines formed between my brow at the thought of her crying while home alone. "The idea of me bringing anyone home other than you is ridiculous, I'm begging, baby, hear me this once, when I say I only want you."

She laughed. "I can get used to listening to you say that."

I pressed our foreheads against each other. "You're sure you'll be okay when I have to leave again eventually? It won't be often, but I will have to travel on occasion for training and events. Plus the actual event of course."

"Yes, it's no problem. Maybe write me a letter or two for good measure," she joked.

"We'll definitely strive to work on our communication next time." I looked around the apartment we were in. "You sure, baby? Because you kind of flew the coop."

"I'm sure, it was just so weird and sad living there without you. I think it was just the reminder that you were happy without me, and I was just stuck there thinking about you."

"Trust me, there was no happiness, only spiking." She laughed at my serious tone. "All I thought about was you, it killed me to hear you upset and not be there to comfort you."

"I love you," she said again. "I think it's important for our child to see us loving each other. And it's good for us too, to be happy ya know?"

"I love you more." I leaned over and tickled her side.

"It's not a competition," she squealed.

"It's *always* a competition, Finch."

Chapter 26

Reese

Ryan sat next to me, pressed to my side when I remembered. "I have our gender reveal if you want to read it together?"

"What do you mean? I thought you knew and were just waiting to tell me when we were together."

"No, I decided it was only fair to find out together. I had the ultrasound tech write it down for us on a piece of paper." I stood to go to my bag and pulled out what I needed. "Here's our newest picture."

He held the photo carefully and poured over the image. I gave him time to look it over while I watched his reaction. "We need to put this on our fridge," he concluded.

"We'll do it the second we get home." I gave the small envelope to him next. "Ready to do it now? I was planning on getting a cake or something more exciting, but honestly I can't wait any longer."

"Ready. We should open it together." He had one hand on it while I held the other side of the envelope, we pushed up the flap with our thumbs, and I reached in to pull up the small piece of paper inside of it.

I looked at him to make sure he was ready. He looked back at me with a smile and wrapped his arm around me. "Are you hoping for anything?" I asked.

He answered my question with a question. "Is it selfish to say I want a girl?"

"No, as long as you're happy either way. Why a girl?"

He gave me a look like it was a silly question. "I obviously want a mini-you running around. I can't think of anything better. A boy would be okay, though."

My heart skipped a beat at the idea he would want two of me around. Especially after all of the stress I put on him over these past few weeks. I also secretly wanted a girl, if only to right the wrongs that were done to me as a child. The idea of a little Ryan running around was pretty exciting too, though.

"Alright, should we count down?" He nodded, and I kept my hand on the small piece of paper.

"Three," we said in unison.

"Two."

"One," I gasped. "A girl! We're having a girl!" I threw my arms around Ryan and squeezed tight. My eyes hadn't stayed dry for very long during this pregnancy, and today was no different.

"You're happy?" Ryan sounded breathless. I nodded and held his face in my hands.

"So happy." We looked into each other's eyes, and I smiled like a giddy school girl. "We're having a baby girl."

"We are." He leaned down to press a quick kiss to my lips. "Let's get you home so we can properly celebrate."

* * *

238

I sat on the bench at the foot of Ryan's, correction– *our* bed. A week into our official relationship, and we decided to finally join our bedrooms together. We shared a bed every night anyway, it was just a matter of moving my clothes and furniture into Ryan's bedroom since he had the nicer bathroom. I was forbidden from helping though, so I sat comfortably while he lugged clothes and furniture back and forth.

"Still have two perfectly good hands if you need anything," I reminded sarcastically.

He huffed and set down another pile of my clothes on the chair in the corner of the room. "You're *growing* two perfectly good hands just sitting there. You're busy."

I rolled my eyes dramatically and leaned back against the bed. His overprotectiveness annoyed me at first, but now it just felt endearing. If it ever became ridiculous, and sometimes it did, he was willing to compromise to some degree. I started to realize that this was his way of chipping in, and he just wanted to make me happy.

He made another round trip between our rooms and came back with a stack of my books. He placed them on the dresser and went back for more. I watched him come and go with a smile on my face.

His phone ringing stopped him in his tracks. I watched him stare at the screen for a few seconds too long. "Everything okay?" I asked.

"It's the manager from the Olympic team."

I sat up straight. "Do you want me to leave?"

"No, stay." He came over to sit on the bench next to me. He answered the call and set it to speaker. "Hey, Mason."

"Summers," he greeted. "We missed you at the banquet."

239

"Sorry, sir. My girlfriend is pregnant and needed me here."
He looked over at me while he said 'girlfriend' with the
proudest smile on his face. I reached over to squeeze his hand.

The man on the phone continued on in a firm voice, "I
need to know you're committed to this team. I understand,
you've got a family to take care of, but if you're going to be an
Olympian you have to be here when I need you here."

"I understand, sir. We've talked it over, and my girlfriend
and I are prepared for the future. I'm committed to this team."

"That's good to hear. It would be a shame to miss out on
having you playing for our side of the court."

"So I'm in?"

"You're in, I'll send your manager the paperwork in a bit.
Just wanted to tell you myself." I stood up and couldn't help
but do a silent dorky celebration. My smile was ear to ear.

"Thank you, I won't let you down." He kept his voice calm,
but Ryan's smile matched mine.

"And Summers?"

"Yes, sir."

"If you leave in the middle of the night again with no more
than an email, we're going to have problems."

"It won't happen," Ryan assured.

"Good, we'll see you soon then."

He hung up the phone and I dragged him up until he was
standing. "You're going to be an *Olympian*!"

He laughed as shock colored his face. "Yeah, I guess so."

"I'm so proud of you!" I practically jumped on him to hang
from his shoulders. "You did it!"

"Easy, baby." He put his hands under my ass to lift me up,
so I was no longer hanging. "I couldn't have done it without
you."

"Liar," I laughed. "You dirty, rotten liar. That was all you!"

"No, honestly, I was so anxious to get back to you I just wanted to finish every game as quickly as possible. I did some of my best work at that training camp."

"Good to know, maybe you'll be motivated to see us in the crowd when you play the real thing."

He relaxed his shoulders and gave me heart eyes. We stood there in our bedroom, in our home, and smiled at each other. It was overwhelming, the feeling of everything in my life leading up to this very moment. This was the happy ending I saw in books, movies, even in real life. And it was finally mine.

"I love you," Ryan murmured. "More than anything."

I nuzzled my nose against his. "I love you. I love our family, our life. I'm so happy for you."

He nudged my nose to the side and captured my lips in a kiss. He carried us over to our bed and gently placed me down right in the middle. His hand trailed up the inside of my thighs and spread them to fit his body between them.

His lips ghosted over my neck and my breath hitched in my throat. "Reese," he whispered. "I want to take care of you. Will you let me?"

He didn't even need to ask. "Yes." His lips met mine before I even finished getting the word out.

The kiss was sensual, and slow, he was always going so slow. I didn't understand how since we had waited for so much of our lives to do this. A moan slipped past my lips as his tongue slid against mine. My hands slid up his back and into his hair. I pulled on the locks that were just long enough to get a good grip on.

His groan reverberated throughout my body. I loved it when he made noises because of me. I tried pulling him impossibly

241

closer and wrapped my legs around his waist to get better leverage.

His hands slid underneath the hem of my sweater and caressed up my sides. His lips left mine to kiss my jaw, moving back to his favorite spot on my neck and sucking on the skin there. One of his hands left my side to slide down my body to meet my covered pussy.

My gasp spurred him on as he rubbed my clit through my jeans. I felt him smile against my shoulder as my hips lifted to grind against his hand. Chasing that feeling, I couldn't help but spread my legs wider in hopes he would give me more.

"Feeling impatient, baby?" he said while giving me a smug smile. I let out a hurried breath of air and pulled his lips up to meet mine again.

After making me wait far too long, he started tugging my pants down. Clumsily, he moved to my sweater next and pushed it up and over my head. He didn't pause again before taking off my bra and panties in a rush.

Satisfied with his work, he stopped to look at me. There was a certain way Ryan's face darkened with want whenever we were like this. He was always so patient, so soft. But I could tell he wanted anything and everything I could give him.

I couldn't help but glance down at the bulge in his pants as he kept his gaze on me. He pushed up to sit on his knees, hovering over me. "Fuck, Reese," he grunted.

His eyes weren't straying from my wet pussy. I could feel my arousal on my thighs already, there was something so sexy about watching him dote on me. Carrying my things into his room and claiming me as his. And then seeing him achieving one of his biggest goals, the Olympics. I was well and thoroughly turned on.

He flicked his eyes back up to mine and held eye contact as he situated his body to lie down between my legs. He licked a stripe up my pussy slowly before sucking at my clit. My hand flew to the back of his head to hold him there.

"Oh my–" I gasped.

He moved slowly, taking his sweet time. Lazy strokes of my clit and around it drove me absolutely mad. I couldn't help but stare. Those dark eyes, the pleasure in them over each of my reactions. His groans when I had an especially vocal reaction to his tongue.

My back arched at the feeling of him groaning against me. He continued his ministrations as I felt two of his fingers tease the entrance of my pussy. My hand moved from the back of his head to his arm. It was too much, felt too good.

He laughed softly at my knee jerk reaction and continued despite my hand gripping onto his forearm, digging my nails into his arm. His mouth went back to my clit to focus on overstimulating it as he pushed his fingers inside of me.

His fingers always felt bigger than I expected. The stretch drove me to arch my back again and tip my hips up to him. He curled his fingers and I was left seeing stars. My toes curled as he repeatedly hit that same spot that made my moans go higher in pitch.

"Right there, huh?" he said into my pussy. His tongue went back to busying itself with my clit. "How does it feel?"

"So," my words were ripped from my mouth as he curled his fingers again. "So good."

His fingers picked up speed, and he continued sucking on my clit until my eyes were rolling. My breaths came out in short, forced bursts between his thrusts. I clenched around him and pushed and pulled at him all at the same time.

"Come on, baby. Cum for me."

His words pushed me over the edge, and I felt my entire body tense before the ultimate release. He continued his movements through my orgasm until I used both hands to push his head away to stop him licking my pussy.

"Fuck," I breathed. He pulled his fingers out of me and left me a little space to catch my breath. He looked as wrecked as I felt, his hair messed up from my hands and his face covered in my arousal.

He wiped off his mouth with the back of his hand and got to work on his own clothes. His pants pulled down to reveal his hard cock. I was allowed a few seconds to stare before he grabbed my ankles and pulled me to the edge of the bed in a swift tug.

"Do you want this, baby?" He looked back down at my pussy and smirked. "She definitely does."

I couldn't help but laugh at his cockiness. "Yes, I want you."

He lined himself up with my entrance and pushed his dick in slowly. My nails went into his shoulders, surely making angry red lines for him to remember this later. The stretch of his fingers did nothing to prepare me for this.

"Ryan," I whined. He buried himself inside me as slowly as possible. My hips canted up to encourage him more.

"You're doing so good for me, baby," he encouraged. "Taking me so well."

We both groaned together as he bottomed out. I was practically panting already. His head fell to my chest and I felt his arms tighten around me. His restraint seemed to be wearing out, and I was happy for him to finally go a bit faster.

"Fuck me," I begged.

That was all he needed. I felt every inch of him as he thrusted in and out of me, his hot mouth placing kisses randomly across my chest. One of his hands snaked behind my back up to hold the back of my neck. I was securely in place, held between his strong arms as he fucked me.

Moans ripped from my throat, so I tried to bury my face in his shoulder. He backed up immediately, staring at me in my eyes as he repeatedly hit that same spot that made me see stars. Nothing had ever felt this good in my entire life, not even when we fucked the first time. His hips moved in the perfect rhythm, driving me to the edge.

"Holy shit, Reese," he moaned. His eyes found mine again and I felt tears welling up in my eyes. There were so many emotions building up in my body all at once.

My orgasm started rising within me and I could only drop my mouth open to gape at him. My nails found their way from his shoulders to his neck as I hoped to get him closer. My ankles were fully crossed behind his back, my feet pushing his hips into mine.

"You gonna cum again, baby?" he asked. "I'm going to cum right in this cunt, you're having my baby. Maybe we can make it two."

The dirty thought made my back arch into him further. My face pressed against his neck as I moaned without restraint. "Fuck, please."

My cunt clenched around him as my orgasm found me. I bit down on his shoulder to quiet my moans, I just wanted to hear him. The unrestrained moan he treated me with in return was worth it. I rode out my high with every part of me curled into him.

His own release came soon after, his head buried in the sheets next to my head as he let out the prettiest moans. "So fucking perfect. I love you," he groaned.

Through my breaths, I smiled and whispered back, "I love you more."

He rested his forehead on mine and pet my cheek with his thumb. "Not possible."

We shared breath for a few beats before he propped himself up. "I'm gonna clean you up, and then we are laying naked in this bed, potentially forever."

"I'm happy with that," I said with a smile.

Chapter 27

Ryan

I didn't know how Reese was still standing. She had been up since six in the morning decorating our house and making food for our baby shower. I did my best to step in and take over where I could, but she had a mission in mind and wanted everything to be perfect.

Her face wore no sign of tiring anytime soon. In fact, she was practically glowing as she held a present Charlotte handed her. "Here, sit with me," I said. I pulled her down into my lap where I was sitting on the couch.

My arms wrapped around her like a seatbelt, ensuring she would stay in place. "Alright, let's see what we have here."

She carefully unwrapped the gift and opened the box to find bottles from our registry along with a little onesie with cherries on it. "This is so cute, thank you!"

I looked over Reese's shoulder to nod at Nick and Charlotte. "Yeah, thank you. We really needed these."

We invited both of our parents to the baby shower. Reese's mom, of course, wouldn't come, and mine was busy with her new fiance that lived on the West Coast. I was stressed out that we wouldn't have any grandparents here for our baby. We were trying to make these milestones as normal as possible for our child.

As I looked around, I realized the last thing we needed were our parents. All of our best friends surrounded us on my giant couch. My sister sat opposite me on an armchair with a giant smile. Georgia and Ruth were to our left, the girl's present in her hands, ready to shove into Reese's lap. Will was in the corner of the room, quietly watching everything.

Ashton sat next to Georgia with their daughter in his arms, smiling proudly at Reese. Nick, constantly moving, picked up trash and wrapping paper as we opened gifts. He hovered nearby Charlotte who was on the edge of the couch, watching us hold up her gift. Behind him was our photo wall, everyone in the room with us was pictured on it. Some pictures were older, dating back to childhood with Penny and me. Others were newer, like the pictures of Reese and I visiting Ash and Georgia at the hospital when Harper was born.

Happy chatter filled the room as sunlight poured in from the windows behind us. My arms tightened around Reese, and I rested my hands on her belly to greet our baby. Our future was bright, undeniably so. Before Lily was even in the world, she had more love surrounding her than I could ever hope for my child.

Reese, the love of my life, was happier than ever. Happy with me. Every smile, hug, kiss, confession of her love for me, leveled me. She made me better, and I would spend the rest of my life repaying her for that.

The ring box in my pocket felt like it was burning a hole. I was content to save my present for later, when we were alone in our beautiful house. Just the two of us.

* * *

"Please sit down for five minutes, I've got this," I insisted for the fifth time.

Reese stood with a trash bag in her hand and was walking outside with it. "I don't mind helping, I just want to get everything back to normal, so we can relax."

I finished sweeping the pile of crumbs I'd cleaned from the living room floor into the dustpan and walked over to stop her at the front door. "I'll take this. Go sit, please. You've been a busybody all day."

She gave me a sour look but handed over the trash bag. I took it out and came back in to find her sitting on the couch and organizing presents we got on the coffee table. At least she was sitting. I'd learned to pick my battles with her.

I left her to her own devices while I went to break down empty boxes in the garage. I pulled the ring out of my pocket before going back inside the house to make sure it hadn't slipped out somehow. Several dreams about messing up the proposal left me paranoid.

After the kitchen was clean, our new gifts were put away in the baby's room, and the furniture was moved back to normal, I collapsed on the couch. Reese laughed at my dramatics and pushed my arm that happened to land partially on top of her.

"I offered to help, you know."

"I know." I sat up slightly to give her a kiss. "That was nice. I wasn't sure what to expect from my first baby shower, but it was fun. I liked your craft idea of painting onesies."

She smiled down at me resting my head on her shoulder. "They turned out surprisingly well, I prepared myself for the worst on that one."

"Yeah, giving a bunch of gym rats paint brushes could have ended badly in hindsight."

Her hand fell to my hair, and her nails gently raked through it. I could die a happy man. "I think it was an amazing first celebration of our child," she confided.

"I agree. Is that why you were so anxious about everything being perfect?"

She nodded with a wince. "I went a little overboard."

"No, I think it was perfect." I sat up and gave her another slow kiss before rubbing her belly. "Lily is lucky to have you as her mom."

She smiled and gave me another small peck. Her head bent to shyly hide in my shoulder, and I moved to rub her back and pull her closer. "I'm lucky to have you."

I chuckled into her hair. It was definitely the other way around. "Are you in the mood to go hang outside for a bit, or do you want to take a nap?"

We recently got furniture for our little backyard. A table with comfortable chairs to lounge in, and we found ourselves out there a lot now, often watching the cats run around. What Reese didn't know, was I also got those string lights she mentioned wanting and hung them up around the patio.

"Let's go hang out outside. It's a little late for a nap, and we can watch the sunset."

I reached for her hands and helped her up. These days, she waddled more than walked, but I was happy to take it slow. I would be lying if I said I didn't secretly love seeing her pregnant. She was annoyed at her lack of mobility, but I was happy to help her in any way she needed. And she looked fucking adorable.

I opened the sliding glass doors, and she gasped as she

walked through them. "When did you do this?"

"This morning," I answered while bending down on one knee. She stared up at the lights in awe, only to turn around and find me kneeling before her. Her hands flew to cover her mouth as it gaped open.

My heart was beating out of my chest, and I wasn't entirely sure I wasn't going to pass out. My palms grew sweaty as I fumbled around pulling the ring out of my pocket and opened it up in front of her.

"Reese Elizabeth Finch, you are the love of my life. My best friend, my greatest joy, and my favorite person all wrapped up in one body. We've spent most of our lives together, and I would love nothing more than to spend the rest of mine waking up next to you. Will you marry me?"

Tears flowed down her face as she nodded and fanned herself before squeaking, "Yes!"

I reached for her ring finger and slid it on slowly. My hands shook with nerves and the overwhelming excitement of knowing she said yes. She let out a wet laugh as she looked at the ring. I laughed too, more out of relief than anything.

"It's beautiful," she muttered.

I stood up to be closer to her and pulled her into a hug. It was a long hug, and I felt her crying against me. I pulled back to lift up her face to look at her. "I'm glad you like it."

"It really is so beautiful," she whispered while looking at me. I wiped tears away from her face.

"I'm really glad you said yes." I reached into my other back pocket to pull out a piece of paper. I handed it to her and gave her just enough space to open it. "It seemed a little less romantic to catch you on a technicality."

She unfolded the worn piece of paper to find our marriage

contract that we drafted in high school. "Oh my god, how did you get this?"

"I have my ways."

Her thumb brushed over our writing that was surrounded by some mathematical algorithm I'd forgotten years ago. She let out a burst of happy laughter. "Did you change the date?"

I looked at the paper to see the date she was referring to. There, a significantly darker writing covered the original date that would have been in a little under two years, with today's date. I gave past me a pat on the back for only using pencil on such an important document.

"I'm not sure if that can be proven or not."

She looked up at me again, and we shared a love-stricken smile. "I can't wait to be Reese Summers."

I nearly groaned at the thought. Gently wrapping my arms under her, I lifted her up to bring her over to a chair to sit down together. We sat there, watching the sunset. It was one of the most beautiful sunsets that I'd ever seen. My eyes mostly stayed on Reese despite the natural wonder. She was my dream turned into reality. My ring on her finger glinted in the sun, and I let out a deep breath that I had held in for years.

Epilogue

Reese

"Daddy, why are we hiding?"

"We're surprising Mommy, keep your head down, princess," Ryan's deep voice could be heard from the entryway. I kicked off my shoes and put on my best poker face, pretending like I hadn't heard a thing.

"Hellooo. Is anyone home?" I called dramatically.

Silence and a few muffled giggles echoed back at me. "Where is my family?" I stalked around our first floor, moving through the kitchen, garage, and dining room. Giggles got louder as I circled around back to the living room, where a suspiciously large pile of blankets peeked up behind the couch.

"Lily? Ryan? Did you guys leave me?" More girlish giggles spilled out behind the blanket. I quietly perched on the couch and reached for the blanket covering their heads. Swiftly, I pulled it straight up and uncovered them.

"Hey!" I accused. "Were you guys hiding from me?"

More squeals of laughter filled the room as I lifted Lily to sit on the couch with me. Ryan stood and kissed my hair before walking around and sitting next to us.

"Sorry, we weren't sure if you were a monster or not."

"A monster? Do I look like a *monster* to you?" More peals of giggles.

"If you are, you're the most beautiful monster I've seen," Ryan said with a smirk before leaning in and giving me a quick peck.

"Gross," Lily said while still laughing. She pushed him away from us and snuggled back into my arms. Lately, she was in a cooties phase and disliked anytime we showed physical affection to each other.

"How was your day?" Ryan asked.

"Good," I said while brushing back Lily's hair. Her bountiful curls definitely came from me, but her dark brown eyes that glimmered with light were all Ryan's. "We made macaroni art today."

"What's that?" Lily asked.

"It's an arts and craft, maybe we can do it together sometime?" She nodded and returned her focus to a beaded bracelet I was wearing. Ryan reached out and brushed his hand against my other arm. I watched him watching me with fondness and asked, "Did you two have a fun day?"

"Absolutely, we made the cats a new house outside." His newfound love of construction and handiwork never failed to amaze me. He was *such* a dad, and I loved every second of it. "Lily painted some very nice flowers on it."

"And bad guys," our sweet four year old added.

I gave Ryan a look. Our daughter had a strange obsession with villains, she wasn't scared of them. In fact, she admired them. Often wanting to collect toys for the 'bad guys' in her favorite stories than the heroes.

"That's fun, I'm sure the cats will appreciate the extra protection and decoration. Maybe when Daddy goes to training next we can make a little garden to go in front of their house."

"Why do you have to wait for me to be gone?" he said, sounding offended.

Lily's head spun to look up at me with a smile. She loved nothing more than ganging up on her dad to tease him. "No offense love, but you kill plants just by looking at them."

"I do not."

Lily laughed and pointed at him. "You watered a cactus," she mimicked words during my laughing fit when I lost my mind a few months ago over his ability to kill even a tiny cactus in our windowsill by overwatering it.

"At least I can tie my shoes," Ryan murmured.

I furrowed my brow and gave him a look for trying to show up our four year old *child*.

* * *

"Night night," Lily called for the third time.

"Goodnight," I echoed. I nudged Ryan with my elbow and left the door cracked until he said it too, "Goodnight, Lil."

I shut the door softly before she could start another conversation and distract us to prolong her bedtime any further. "She is so your daughter," he whispered with a snicker. "You could put a scarecrow in her room, and she'd talk to it for hours."

"She loves us, you fall for it just as much as I do."

He sighed with a content smile, "I do."

We made our way downstairs and sat on the couch together, my legs in Ryan's lap and his arms around my waist. I sighed and sunk deeper into him. For the first time since this morning, the house was completely quiet.

This was the best part of my day. Sure, I still had my coffee in the mornings (sometimes Ryan even made it for me now, the *right* way), but laying down with my husband in our home after a long day was the best. His hand subconsciously went to the ring on my finger to rub at it.

"I have a surprise for you," he murmured.

I sat up a little to look up at him. "What for?"

"It's our alternate reality anniversary." I let out a soft laugh. Every year we celebrated our anniversary full out, since we both agreed our relationship was one of our greatest achievements in life. We always did presents, a date night, the whole nine yards.

But, Ryan also liked to keep track of another date. The original date on our silly marriage contract that meant we would have gotten married when I was 30 and he was 28. It was exactly halfway between our birthdays, and he never forgot. I asked him why, he referred to it as the inevitable, that we always would've ended up together, even if the events happened slightly differently. So, it was important to be happy for our alternate reality selves on their anniversary too.

"How are we celebrating this year?"

He pulled my hand up to kiss our wedding ring. "I got a cake. I figured we could keep it nice and simple."

"Oooh, what kind?"

"Chocolate, of course." Without warning, he stood up with his hands underneath me. Carrying me in his strong arms, he walked to the kitchen and placed me down on a stool. He moved the chocolate cake from the counter top to the island in front of me. It was beautiful and looked absolutely mouth watering.

"I love you," I said. It was so easy to love him. Our lives fit together perfectly, and I thought of past me, who was so worried about everything not working out. She needed time and patience, which Ryan gave tenfold. Over the years, I learned to trust. And my life was so much better for it.

"I love you more," Ryan answered. He placed a slice of cake in front of me and sat down. Seconds later, he stood slightly as he moved his stool to be even closer to me. Our thighs brushed against each other, and I laughed at his blatant love for physical affection.

We each got a bite of cake on our forks and cheers-ed them. "To always falling for you in every lifetime," he said.

"May alternate Ryan and Reese live a very happy life," I echoed.

Acknowledgement

Thank you for supporting my dream of writing. If you're reading this, you've made a direct impact on my silly little life, so thank you! I hope this book brings you as much joy as it brought me to write it.

I'd also like to give a big shout out to all the fanfic writers, who changed my mind on the accidental pregnancy trope. I am now a proud supporter.

My rescue dog, Poppyseed, Olive, Ollipop, the pup of many names, who always reminds me to live in the moment and take a break from writing, you can't read this, but I love you.

My family, you won't read this, but I appreciate your support of my writing even though I'm private about it. Your excitement over my work means the world. Maybe one day you can read this and laugh!

My writing friends, reading friends, social media pals, I am so so thankful for you. As an indie author and perfectionist, it's easy to doubt my work, but you all keep me going! I love having a community of people who love romance to connect with. To the readers that send a DM after they've finished a book to tell me they loved it, those make my day! Keep it going!

Printed in Great Britain
by Amazon